I0610553

Dorvil Miller Wilcox

Vital Records of Lee, Massachusetts, 1777-1801

from the records of the town, Congregational church and inscriptions in

the early burial grounds - all the family birth records continued beyond

1801 given as fully as recorded

Dorvil Miller Wilcox

Vital Records of Lee, Massachusetts, 1777-1801
*from the records of the town, Congregational church and inscriptions in the early
burial grounds - all the family birth records continued beyond 1801 given as fully as
recorded*

ISBN/EAN: 9783337193263

Printed in Europe, USA, Canada, Australia, Japan

Cover: Foto ©Andreas Hilbeck / pixelio.de

More available books at **www.hansebooks.com**

VITAL RECORDS OF LEE

MASSACHUSETTS

1777-1801

FROM THE

RECORDS OF THE TOWN

CONGREGATIONAL CHURCH

AND

NSCRIPTIONS IN THE EARLY BURIAL GROUNDS

ALL THE FAMILY BIRTH RECORDS CONTINUED BEYOND 1801 GIVEN
AS FULLY AS RECORDED

———

ONTAINING ALSO THE BAPTISMS AND NAMES OF CHURCH MEMBERS
IN THE RECORDS OF THE CONGREGATIONAL CHURCH FROM
ITS ORGANIZATION IN 1780 TO 1801

——— ———

Literally Reproduced

——— ———

1899

CONTENTS

The upper part of this page was written by Seen Fowler, Ye deeds out by Nathan Dillingham.

... the town ... with the office or published ... of the Town per me. J B Town Clerk ——

... Willcox Lois goodrich both of Lee ... Published according ... of the Town. Per me. J B Town Clerk

November the 16th 1792 Jared Ingersoll of Lee Elizabeth Nichols of the ... ... were Published according to the Custom of the town per me J B Town Clerk

Lee ... November the 24 AD 1792 Ely Bradley and Phebe Bartlone both of ... ... Published according to the Custom of the Town per me J B Town Clerk

Sunday April 13th 1783 Wm Ingersoll Jr and Marcy Crocker were Published by ... Dillingham ——

Published the following, Jared Smith & Mehittabel Howard
Walter Tiffany & Sally Avery
Levi Hart & Bathsheba Rider — David Baker & ... Crocker —
Peter Willcox Jr & Polly Mansfield — Jesse Bartholomew & Nancy
Bradley — Married May 26 1784
Isaac Grant & Hannah Tracey

Lee October ... 1779 ... the Within named ... & ...
... Joyned in Lawful Wedlock before me Stephen West

Marriages

... Jewish Gate married to Ruth Tracey September 26th 1776.
Nehemiah Smith & Fanny Mansfield, May 28th 1789.
David Foot & Betsey Hamlin — Jany 12th 1789.
Rufus Manton Jr & Rachel Coldey — Feby 18th 1789.
John Green & Martha Hamlin Dec — 1st 1789
Calvin Ingersoll & Lydia Barlow Oct 15th 1789
... Sutherland & Jerusha Stanley Feb — 1790
Samuel Barlow & Beautiful ... Dec 29 — 17..
Oziel Willcox & Lois Goodrich Oct 10..
Sylvenus Gifford & Tabitha Dexter Dec..
Duncan Shaw & Abigail ...
Benj Clark & Sarah ...
Seth ... & ...

INTRODUCTORY NOTES.

The town of Lee, Mass., was formed from parts of Great Barrington and Washington, the Glass Works Grant, and part of Williams's Grant. It was incorporated Oct. 21, 1777, and the first town meeting was held Dec. 26, 1777.

The number of inhabitants at the time of incorporation has been variously estimated from 250 to 350. It is probable that the latter number is more correct. In 1791 the population was 1,170; in 1800 it was 1,267.

The first settlers were mostly from neighboring towns, and from Connecticut. Several families, however, were from Plymouth and Barnstable counties, and several Dutch families from New York, were located on the Hoplands, and Glass Works Grant. Soon after the incorporation, a considerable accession to the population was made by families from Barnstable, Sandwich, Wareham, Falmouth and other Cape towns, where the sea-faring occupations of the people had been partly suppressed by the British during the War of the Revolution, forcing them to seek a subsistence elsewhere.

The publishments and marriages, births and deaths among these pioneers, which are recorded on our town and church records, with also, the few inscriptions in our early burial grounds are gathered into this volume.

The vital records of the town clerks include all entries to the present century, but as the birth records in this town were arranged by families until 1844, when the present uniform system of vital records went into effect in this state, in order to make this department of the records satisfactory, and of use to genealogists, each of these family records is given as completely as recorded — several extending into the third decade of the present century.

The town clerks for the period over which the birth records in the volume extend, were as below, with the term of service of each:—

Prince West was chosen at the first town meeting and served to March 18, 1782, but according to the first two publishments recorded (see p. 1), he acted as such before he was chosen Dec. 26, 1777; Thomas Beecher served from March 18, 1782 to April 7, 1783; Nathan Dillingham from April 7, 1783 to March 4, to 1793, and also from March 7, 1814 to March 4, 1816; Daniel Wilcox from March 4, 1793 to March 3, 1806; Nathaniel

Thayer from March 3, 1806 to March 9, 1807; Cornelius T. Fessenden from March 9, 1807 to March 7, 1814; Ransom Hinman from March 4, 1816 to March 8, 1824.

The records prior to Jan. 24, 1791, were first entered in a make-shift book, from which they were transcribed into a more permanent volume by Mr. John Powers, in accordance with a vote of the town Dec. 20, 1790. The original has not been preserved. The copy appears to be the work of a man of slight education. It abounds in rare orthography and construction, but is in a fairly legible hand. Mainly the records for that period pertain to town meeting transactions, elections for state and county officers, cattle marks, and road surveys;—the vital records received little consideration.

The copied part of the records extends over more than thirteen years from the town's incorporation, and the vital records entered during that time, were the publishments and marriages on the first two and a half pages of this volume, and the following birth records:—

Joseph Freeman Austin, p. 12;

Sarah, Abigail and Rebecca Dillingham, p. 21;

Children of Asahel Dodge, except Samuel p. 21;

Percival record to Hannah, p. 33;

Walker record, excepting death of Caleb, p. 38;

Mary, Prudence, and John Brewster West, p. 39;

Christian and Azuba Wood, p. 42.

The dates of most of the above mentioned births, prove that they were originally recorded by Dillingham, and judging from the peculiar form of entry, it is probable the others were recorded by West.

The only death noted is that of Huldah Walker, in the above mentioned Walker record.

The list of marriages at the bottom of p. 3, was recorded by Nathan Dillingham, and a few birth records are in his writing, also the record of Caleb Walker's death. Several of the publishments of the preceding clerk were recorded by Daniel Wilcox. It is supposed that the record of publishments and marriages by the latter is complete. Most of the birth records herein printed are wholly or in part in his writing.

Wilcox's records are not very plain. Evidently he drove a rapid, and careless quill. In his manuscript small e and i are generally indistinguishable, and the same character often stands for small a, o and u. Altogether his writing is very peculiar. Numerous words are not fully written out, —the most frequent fault in this respect being the omission of a letter or syllable from the end of words. The last peculiarity is not often seen in his vital records, but cler for clerk appears in the last intention on p. 5, and several times also on pp. 7, 8, 9. Some date-errors also appear; as for instance, he records that his brother Oziel was killed at Sheffield, March 27, 1787. Oziel was an adherent of Daniel Shays, and was killed in the skirmish which took place between the insurgents and state forces at Sheffield

Feb. 27, 1787. Other errors of date have been noticed, and where considerable are noted. His record of the death of his brother Peter (p. 46), and of his sister Electa (p. 48), are circumstantial to an extent seldom attempted by town clerks.

The records in Dillingham's own hand, and those by the other clerks, were more carefully written, and probably are more correct.

For further information regarding the birth records, consult note on p. 12, and regarding the record of deaths, consult note on p. 43.

There are doubtless some gaps in the continuity of the church records before Dr. Hyde's pastorate, but the names of all members of the church are mentioned therein, which appear for that period in the first published list (supposed date 1818), except David Baker, and Stephen Tobey, received in 1792. Whether all the baptisms are mentioned, cannot be determined.

The records kept by Dr. Hyde contain a list of all baptisms, admissions to the church, marriages solemnized by him, and deaths in town from June 6, 1792 to the time of his death in 1833. His records herein printed are limited to the close of the year 1800.

The matter from both the town and church records, has been carefully printed from the original manuscripts — the spelling, abbreviations, and punctuation being exactly given, and since it was printed has been compared with the original, and all typographical errors, which have been discovered, have been corrected or are noted among the errata on p. 108.

All the inscriptions antedating 1801 in the early burial grounds are carefully reproduced, and the marriages of some Lee people recorded in other towns, are given in the appendix; also several family records inadvertently omitted from the records of births, pp. 12-42.

The reason the volume is limited to so short a period of the town's existence is that it has been for the most part printed from forms for a larger book which contains all the extant records of the town officers, Congregational church, Hopland School District, etc., for the same period,—a few necessary changes of type having been made.

It was thought a few copies containing only the matter herein given, might be of value for local use, and for genealogical libraries, and so it was proposed to print 150 copies, but in printing, several extra sheets were struck off — the whole being 158.

Publishments and Marriages.

December 16th AD: 1777 then Was Noah Burdin of Lee and Avis Th* * * † of Chesterfield Was Published According to Law by me Prince West Town Clark —

December 22d AD: 1777 then Was Ichabod Backus and Deliverance Hamlin both of Lee Was Published According to Law by me Prince West Town Clark —

February 2d AD: 1778 then Was Amos fuller of Skeenborough and Anne Huggins of Lee Was Published as the Law Directs By me Prince West Town Clark —

March 19th AD: 1778 then Jacob Pratt of great Barington and Meribah Chanter of Lee Was Published as the Law Directs By Prince West Town Clark

March 19th 1778 Jacob Pratt and Meribah Chanter Was Joyned in Lawful Wedlock By me Jah! Woodbridge Jus? Peace

Lee March 25th A D: 1778 then Receiv'd and Recorded the above By me Prince West Town Clark

April 6th AD: 1778 then Jesse Clark and Sarah foot Both of Lee Was Published as the Law Directs ꝑr me Prince West Town Clark

July 28th AD: 1778 then the Intention of Marage Between George Chanter of Lee and Martha Owen of great Barington Was made Publick ꝑr me Prince West

Sep? 24 AD: 1778 then the Intention of Marage Between Constant Bozworth of Sanderfield [and] Marcy West was made Publick as the Law Directs Pr me Prince West

December 20 AD: 1778 then the intention of Marage Between Samuel Wright of Lee and Jemininiah Hencock of Springfield Was made Publick as the Law Directs Pr me Prince West ‡

January 20 AD: 1779 then was Published george Adkins and Sarah Dimmuck as the Law Directs Pr me Prince West —

† Record mutilated, —see ꞏ ꞏ ꞏ?.

‡ "The intention of Marriage between Sam!! Wright of Lee and Jemima Hancock of Springfield are here entered Novr 30th anno Domini 1778 Notification posted ye 5th Day of Decr following"

Springfield Records of Marriages, Vol. 2, Page 210.
I find no record of the marriage of the above named persons.
[Signed,]   E. A. Newell, City Clerk. [1897.]

Orasha Strong and Pasahance Stevens Was Published as the Law Directs february 20th AD: 1779 Pr me Prince West ——

february 20 AD: 1779 Timothy Treat of Lenox and Bulah Strong of Lee Was Published as the Law Directs Pr me Prince West ——

Published March the 1st AD: 1779 the Intention of Marage Between Orasha Strong and Patiance Stevens Both of Lee as the Law Directs Prince West

March 4th 1779 The Within Named Orasha Strong and Patience Stevens Was Joyned in Lawful Wedlock Before me Stephen West

a True Copy atested By me Prince West Town Clark ——

Published March the 3d AD: 1779 fenner foot and sarah Willcox Both of Lee Pr me Prince West Clark

March the 11th 1779 the Within named fenner foot and Sarah Willcox was Joyned in Lawful Wedlock Before me Stephen West

a true Coppy Tested by me Prince West Town Clark

Published August 20 AD: 1779 francis Nye And Meriam Dodge Both of Lee as the Law Directs By me Prince West Town Clark

Lee Sepr 2d 1779 the Within Name[d] francis Nye and Meriam Dodge was Joyned in Lawful Wedlock before me Stephen West

a True Copy Attest By me Prince West Town Clark

Lee October 10th AD: 1779 then Intention of Marage Between John Nye of Lee and Louis West of Tolland has been published as the Law directs

Lee October 12 AD: 1779 then the Intention of Marage Between Ebenezer West of Lee and Mehitibel Nye of Wilingtown Was Published as the Law Directs

Lee October 13th 1779 then the Within Named Seth Nye and Ama West Ware Joyned in Lawful Wedlock before me Stephen West ——

Lee June 20th AD: 1780 the Day Aaron Wormer and Pheba Vallet * * * † Published as the Law Directs Pr me Prince West ——

October Published Lewis Hatch of Lee and Mary Davis of Lee Pr me Prince West T Clark

November 24 AD: 1780 Nathaniel Gillet of Newlebenon [and] Sibbel Calkins of * * * † Published Pr me Prince West Town Clark

December 3 AD: 1780 Published Amasiah Dotty of Plimtown and Bathiah Hamlin of Lee By me Prince West Town Clark

December 10 AD: 1780—Published John haas of Kinderhoock and ficha Howk of Lee Pr me Prince West

Lee March 19 AD: 1782 Nathaniel Toby and Deborah finney Was Published as the Law Directs Pr me Prince West

The Within Named Nathaniel Toby & Deborah finney Ware Joyned in Lawful Wedlock Before me Wm Ingersoll Justice of the Peace

March 21 AD: 1782

† Record mutilated.

Lee 1782 Solomon Davis [and] Martha Mansfield Both of Lee are Published According to the Custom of the Town Pr me T B T C

Lee 1782 Jedediah Crocker and Sarah Gifford both of Lee are published According to the Custom of the Town pr me T B Town Clark ——

Lee 1782 Ozial Willcox [and] Lois goodrich both of Lee are Published According to the Custom of the Town Pr me T B Town Clark

[See below for marriage.]

Lee November the 16th 1782 Jared Ingersoll of Lee Elizarbeth Nibelow of Sharron are Published According to the Custom of the town pr me T B Town Clark

Lee November the 24 AD: 1782 Ely Bradley and Phebe Bartiline Both of Lee Are Published According to the Custom of the Town Pr me T B— Town Clark

Sunday April 13th 1783 Wm Ingersoll Jur and Marcy Crocker were Published by N Dillingham

Published the following, Isral Smith & Mehettabel Howard
                         Walter Tiffany & Sally Avery ——
                         Levi West & Bathshua Rider ——
                         David Baker & Vina Crocker ——
                         Peter Willcox Jr & Polly Mansfield ——
                         Jesse Bartholomew & Mamry Bradley ——
Married May 26th 1784—Isaac Grant & Hanah Tracey

[The foregoing Publishments and Marriages are in the writing of John Powers. copyist —— The following list of Marriages is in Nathan Dillingham's writing:]

Marriages.

Capt Josiah Yale married to Ruth Tracey Septemr 26th 1776. ——
Nehemiah Smith & Fanny Mansfield, May 28th 1789.
David Foot & Betsey Hamlin —— Jany — 12th 1789.
Rufus Stanton Jr & Rachel Eddey - Octr 18th 1789.
John Green & Martha Hamlin Decr 1st 1789
Calvin Ingersoll & Lydia Barlow Octr 8th 1789
John Sutherland & Jerusha Stanley Feb— 1790
Lemuel Barlow & Thankful Bassett Dec. 23d 1785
Oziel Willcox & Lois Goodrich Octr 10th 1782
Sylvenus Gifford & Tabitha Dexter Decr 2d 1790
Duncan Shaw & Abigail Gifford - Jan. 6th 1791
. Benja Clark & Sarah Cole both of Lenox Sepr -1-1790
Seth Barden & Bethiah Dimmuck Decr 19th 1790 ——

4

[The records of the following Publishments and Marriages are in Daniel Wilcox's writing.]

The intention of Marriage between Jonathan Walley of Richmond and Mary Winslow of Lee was made public July 18th 1792 by Nathn Dillingham   And married by Revd Alvan Hyde July 19th 1792

The intention of marriage between Ebenr Jenkins Jr & Lydia Smith both of Lee was made public August 9th 1792 by Nathan Dillingham T. Clerk   And married by Revd Alvan Hyde Augt 23d 1792

The intention of marriage between Heman Bradley & Anne West both of Lee was made publick August 28th 1792 by Nathn Dillingham T. Clerk And married by Rev'd Alvan Hyde Novr 29th 1792

The intention of marriage between Josiah Willoughby & Sally Backus both of Lee was made public October 16th 1792 by Nathan Dillingham T. Clerk   And married by Revd Alvan Hyde Octr 18 1792 —

The intention of marriage between Joshua Nye & Charta Parker both of Lee was made public Novr 18th 1792 by Nathan Dillingham T. Clerk And married by Revd Alvan Hyde Novr 20th 1792

The intention of marriage between Walley Backus & Grace Vandusen both of Lee was made public Jany 17th 1793 by Nathan Dillingham T. Clerk   And married by Revd Alvan Hyde Jany 17th 1793

The intention of marriage between Ichabod L[a]throp of Anodaque & Esther Pixley of Lee was made public Jan,y 31—1793 by Nathan Dillingham T. Clerk   And married by Rev,d Alvan Hyde Jany 31—1793

The intention of marriage between Aneel Bassett & Hannah Dimmuck was made public March 1st 1793 by Nathan Dillingham T. Clerk and married by the Revd Alvan Hyde Apl 11th 1793

The intention of marriage between Rev'd Alvan Hyde of Lee and Lucy Fessenden of Sandwich were made public April 4th 1793 by D Willcox T. C   And married by Rev'd Stephen West Apl 25th 1793 ——

The intention of Marriage between Asael Foot & Anne Abbot was made public Aug.20th 1793 by Danl Willcox T. Clerk.   And married by the Rev'd Alvan Hyde Aug.21st 1793. ——

The intention between Jabez Bursley & Abigail Perry both of Lee were made public June 30 1793 by Danl Willcox T. C.   A[nd] married by the Revd Alvan Hyde Octr 17th 1793 ——

The intention of marriage between Joseph Whiton & Amanda Garfield were made public Octr 11th 1793 by Danl Willcox T. C. And married by the Revd Alvan Hyde Octr 17th 1793 ——

The intention of marriage between Pardon Austin of Tyringham and Rhoda Stanton of Lee was made public Novr 28th 1793 by Danl Willcox T. C. and married the same evening by the Revd Alvan Hyde

The intention of Marriage between Crispus Shaw & Levina Shaw both of Lee was made public Feby 24th 1794 by Daniel Willcox T. Clerk and married by Eben^r Jenkins Esq May 8th 1794

The intention of marriage between Jacob Penoyer & Alice Hoyt Crocker both of Lee was made public March 21 1794 by Dan! Willcox T Clerk and married March 27th 1794 by the Revd Alvan Hyde

The intention of marriage between Eph^m Sheldon of Stockbridge and Lydia Gifford of Lee was made public May 25th 1794 by Dan! Willcox T. C. and married the Same Evening by the Revd Alvan Hyde. †

The intention of Marriage between Silas Easton of East Hartford and Rachel Nye of Lee was made public June 25th 1794 by Dan! Willcox T. C. and married by the Revd Alvan Hyde June 30th 1794 ——

The intention of Marriage between Daniel Willcox & Lydia Ball both of Lee was made public June — 1794 and married on the Sabbath October 19th 1794 by the Revd Alvan Hyde ——

The intention of marriage between Isaac Barlow and Sally Casey both of Lee was made public July 6th 1794 and married July 8th 1794 by the Revd Alvan Hyde

The intention of marriage was made public July 20th 1794 between Joseph Hinkley and Polly Stewart both of Lee by Dan! Willcox T. C. and Married Novr 19th 1794 by A. Hyde

The intention of marriage between Stephen Dexter & Lydia Backus both of Lee was made public July 21st 1794 by D. Willcox T. Clerk and married by the Revd Alvan Hyde Octr 24th 1794 —

The intention of marriage between David Hamlin and Sally Backus both of Lee was made public July 28th 1794 by D. Willcox T. C & married October 8th 1794 by Revd Alvan Hyde

The intention of marriage between John Read of Stockbridge & Elizabeth Crocker of Lee was made Public Aug. 18th 1794 by D. Willcox T. Clerk and married Aug. 24th 1794 by the Revd Alvan Hyde — ‡

The intention of marriage between Abraham Finney and & Huldah Gifford both of Lee was made public Septr 17th 1794 by Dan! Willcox T. Clerk and married by the Revd Alvan Hyde Novr 20th 1794

The intention of marriage between Israel Thompson of Goshen & Sally Foot of Lee was made public as the Law directs October—1794 by Dan! Willcox T. Cler

† In the Record of Marriages, Stockbridge, for 1794 is the following entry: "Ephraim Sheldon and Lydia Gifford of Lee were married May 25th."

‡ "John Read and Elizabeth Crocker of Lee were married August 24th." Ibid.

The intention of marriage between Josiah Crocker and Hannah Crosby both of Lee was made public October 27th 1794 by Danl Willcox T. Clerk and married Jany 15th 1795 by Revd Alvan Hyde

The intention of marriage between Abijah Crosby & Caty Olds both of Lee was made public Novr 20th 1794 by Danl Willcox T. Clerk and married January 15th 1795 by Revd Alvan Hyde ——

The intention of marriage between Lemi Bradley of Lee, and Ruth Newel of Lenox was made public Feb. 18th 1795 by Danl Willcox T. C- and married Feb.19th 1795 by the Revl Alvan Hyde +

The intention of marriage between Benjamin Hamlin & Thankful Barlow both of Lee was made public Feb. 18th 1795 by D. Willcox T. Clerk and married Feb. 19th 1795 by the Revd Alvan Hyde ——

The intention of marriage between Reuben Pixley Jr and Polly Chase both of Lee was made public June 1795 and Married June 1795 by the Revd Alvan Hyde ——
[On the next page of the Records is another entry of the same, as follows:]
The intention of marriage between Reuben Pixley Jr & Polly Chase both of Lee was made public June 2d 1795 by Danl Willcox T. C- and married by Revd Alvan Hyde June 3d 1795 ——

Married June 27th 1795 Nathl Gleason & Polly Patman both of Becket by Ebenr Jenkins Esq

The intention of marriage between William Sturges and Sallome Dimmuck both of Lee was made public Aug 31st 1795 by Danl Willcox T. Clerk   Married Septr 10th 1795 by Revd Alvan HyDE
[On the next page of the Records is the following entry of the same:]
The intention of marriage between Wm Sturges and Salome Dimuck both of Lee was made public Aug. 31 1795 by D. willcox T C — and married by Revd Alvan Hyde Septr 11th 1795

The intention of marriage between Stephen Johnston of Tyringham & Rebecca Clark of Lee was made public Aug. 31st 1795 by Danl Willcox T. Clerk

The intention of marriage between Hope Davis and Lucy Bullard both of Lee was made public Septr 7th 1795 by Danl Willcox T. Clerk and married the same day by the Revd Alvan Hyde
[On the next page of the Records is the following entry:]
This may Certify that the intention of marriage between Hope Davis & Lucy Bullard both of Lee was made public Septr 7th 1796 by D. Willcox T- C — and married the same day by Revd Alvan Hyde ——

The intention of Marriage between Ichabod Sherman of Woodbury (Connecticut) and Avice Collins of Lee was made public Jany 3d 1796 l y D. Willcox T. Clerk ——

† "1795, Feb. 4. Lemi Bradley of Lee and Ruth Newel of Lenox."
From Lenox T. R., Book 1 (original), page 363 under Intentions.

The intention of Marriage between Lewis Gifford of Lee and Betsy Backus of Lee was made public Jany 1796   by D. W. T Cler and married Jany 22 1797 by Revd Alvan Hyde ——

The intention of Marriage between Nathl Hudson of Grenville and Nabby Hinkley of Lee was made public Feb. 1796 by Danl Willcox T Clerk and married June 28th 1796 by the Revd Alvan Hyde
[On the next page of the Records is the following entry of the same:]
The intention of marriage between Nathl Hudson of Grenville and Nabby Hinkley was made public Feb. 4th 1796 by D W. T Clerk and married June 28 1796 by Revd Alvan Hyde ——

The intention of marriage between Reuben Penoyer & Polly Gifford both of Lee was made public Feb. 9th 1796 by D. Willcox T. C — and married March 19th 1796 by Revd Alvan Hyde

The intention of marriage between Paul Ewer & Susannah Hamblin both of [Lee] was made public Feb. 16th 1796 by D. Willcox T. Clerk and Married by Revd Alvan Hyde Feb. 18th 1796

The intention of marriage between Benjn Adams & Sarah Parker both of Lee was made Public March 10th 1796 by D. Willcox T. C — and married by Revd Alvan Hyde on the same Evening

The intention of marriage between Jacob Winegar & Anne Parker both of Lee was made public June— 1796 by Danl Willcox T. Clerk Married by Revd Alvan Hyde Novr 1796

The intention of marriage between Moses Ingersoll of Lee & Prudence Taylor of Tyringham was made public July 8th 1796 by Daniel Willcox T. Clerk

The intention of marriage between Simn Wright of Rutland & Susanna Abbot of Lee, made public Novr 8th 1796—married Nov. 8th 1796

The intention of marriage between Ozias Judd & Lucena Hulett both of Lee was made public Novr 27th 1796 by D. Willcox T. Clerk and married by Revd Alvan Hyde Decr 15—1796

The intention of marriage between Ephm Williams & Jemima Wormer both of Lee was made public Decr 4—1796 by D. W. T. Cler and married by Revd Alvan HYDE Jany 26—1797 ——

The intention of marriage between Saml Winegar & Tabitha Crocker both of Lee was made public Decr 11th 1796 by D. Willcox T. Clerk and married by Rev.d Alvan Hyde Jany 12th 1797

The intention of marriage between Harvey Osborn of Royal-Grant and Caty Gifford of Lee was made public Decr 15th 1796 by D. W. T. Clerk —
Married by Revd Alvan Hyde Decr 25th 1796

The intention of marriage between Nathⁿ Bassett & Azuba Jones both of Lee was made public Decr 25th 1796 by D. Willcox T. Clerk and married by Revd Alvan Hyde Jany 12—1797

The intention of Marriage between Peleg Barlow & Esther Griffin both of Lee was ma[de] public Jany 1st 1797 by D. Willcox T. Clerk and married by Revd Alvan Hyde Jany 19th 1797

The intention of marriage between Nathan Ball J^r and Fear Chadwick b[o]th of Lee was m[a]de public Jany 8th 1797 by Danl Willcox T. Clerk and married by Rev^l Alvan Hyde June 29th 1797

The intention of marriage between Benjⁿ Bassett of Tyringham and Molly Winslow of Lee was m[a]de public Jany 8th 1797 by D. Willcox T. Cler and Married Jany 23 1797 by Jo^s Avery ——

The intention of Marriage between Zina Hinkley and B[e]tsey Ball both of Lee was made public Feb. 26—1797 by D. Willcox T Cler Married June 29th 1797 by Revd Alvan Hyde

The intention of Marriage between Job Northrup of Lenox & Sally Bennet of Lee was made Public Septr 10th 1797 by D. Willcox T. C. Married Octr 19th 1797 by Rev^d A Hyde †

The intention of Marriage between Jer[e]h Vallet & Abiah M[o]tt b[o]th of Lee was m[a]de Public Septr 10th 1797 by D. Willcox T. Cler Married Octr 4th 1797 by Revd Alvan Hyde

The intention of Marriage between Wm Foot of Stockbridge and Abia Vallet of Lee was made public Septr 10 h 1797 by D. W. T. Cler Married Novr 9th 1797 by Revd Alvan Hyde ‡

The intention of marriage between Danl Parker of Sandisfield & Anne Handy of Lee was made public Septr 17—1797 by D. Willcox T. Cler Married Novr 23. 1797.

The intention of marriage between Az[e]l H[u]ntington & Hannah Robinson both of Lee was made O[c]t^r 15—1797 by D. Willcox T. Cler

The intention of marriage between John Hulett of Lee & Hannah Walker of Tyringham was made public Octr 22—1797

The intention of marriage between Joseph Frarey of Becket and Sally Gifford made public Octr 29 h 1797—Married Decr 28 1798 [1797]

The intention of marriage between Wm Bradley & Tabitha Hamblin both of Lee was made public Decr 17—1797 Married Jany 3^d 1798 by Revd Alvan Hyde

† This intention entered also, on the Lenox Rec[o]rds, Book 1 (original), page 3[5].
‡ "William Foot and Abia Vallet of Lee were m[a]rried Nov[e]mb[e]r 9th by R[e]v. Alvan Hyde." Stockbridge Records.

The intention of marriage between Calvin Davis & Hannah Crocker both of Lee was made public Dec' 17—1797 by D. W
Married Feb. 1st 1798 by Rev'd Alvan Hyde

The intention of marriage between Levi Fowler of Stockbridge and Silence Chase of Lee was made public Feb. 4th 1798 by Dan! Willcox T. Cler   married Feb. 22d 1798 by Eben' Jenkins Esq +

The intention of marriage between Elisha Dodge & Betsey Crosby both of Lee, made public Apl 15—1798 married June 21st 1798 by Rev'd A. Hyde

The intention of marriage between John White Jr of Norton, & Fear Perry of Lee, made public June 17—1798 by D. Willcox T. Cler—
Married Dec' 13th 1798 by Rev'd Alvan Hyde

The intention of marriage between Alvan Foot of Lee & Sally Percival of Lenox made public June 24th 1798 by D. Willcox T. Cler. ‡

The intention of marriage between Joshua West of Lee and Mary Newell of Lenox made public Aug. 5th 1798 by D. Willcox T. Cler ‡‡

The intention of marriage between Elijah Kilborn of Lee & Lydia Tooley of Gt Barrington made public Nov' 25 1798
Married Jany 3d 1799 by Rev'l A Hyde

The intention of marriage between Oliver Wedge of Litchfield and Martha Grant of Lee, made public Nov' 25 1798
Married Dec' 20th 1798 by Rev'd Alvan Hyde

The intention of marriage between Luther Day of Granville & Meribah Smith of Lee made public Dec' 1798
Married May 12 1799 by Rev'l A Hyde

The intention of marriage between Lodowick Gardner & Hannah Vallet both of Lee made public Dec' 6th 1798

The intention of marriage between Luther Ingersoll of Lee & Betsey Gardner of Tyringham made public Dec' 15th 1798

The intention of marriage between Andrew Howk & Betsey Mansfield made public Feb. 24th 1799   Married March 21 1799 by Rev A Hyde

The intention of mariag between John Gardner of Tyringham & Delia Childs of Lee, made public Apl 14th 1799
Married Sept' 22 1799 by Rev A Hyde

The intention of marriage between Levi Church of Lee, & Hannah Gardner of Tyringham, made public June 2. 1799.

+ "Levi Fowler and Silence Chase of Lee were married Feb. 22nd, 1798 by Ebenezer Jenkens Esq."   Stockbridge Records.

‡ "By Rev. Samuel Shepard—Alvan Foot of Lee to Sarah Percival of Lenox September 27 h, 1798."   Lenox T. R., Book 1 (original), p. 340.

‡‡ "By Rev. Samuel Shepard—Joshua West of Lee to Mary Newel of Lenox September 11th, 1798."   Ibid., p. 341.

The intention of marriage between Thomas Chadwick & Larinda Ingersoll both of Lee made public June 9th 1799.
Married Septr 16 1799 byRev{d} A Hyde

The intention of marriage between Eli Church of Lanesborough & Elizabeth Chadwick of Lee made public Octr 6th 1799.
Married Feby 6 1800 by Revd A Hyde

The intention of marriage between Timothy Thatcher of Lee and Dorothy Phelps of Hebron (Connect) made public Octr 1799

The intention of marriage between Jeduthan West & Phebe Willcox both of Lee made public Decr 29th 1799
Married Ap{l} 24th 1800 by Revd A Hyde

The intention of marriage between Simeon Clark & Lucy Backus both of Lee made Public Jany 5th 1800.
Married by Revd Alvan Hyde Jany 26—1800

The intention of marriage between Saml Barlow & Sena Wilcox both of Lee made public Ap{l} 5th 1800   Married May 1 1800

The intention of marriage between Cornel{s} Fessenden & Nancy Ball both of Lee made public Ap{l} 1800
Married Aug. 8th 1800 by Revd Alvan Hyde

The intention of marriage between John Rathbun & Celia Toby both of Lee made public May 4th 1800   Married June 26 1800 by Rv. A Hyde

The intention of marriage between Benjn Davis of Tyringham & Thankful Hamblin of Lee made public May 11th 180)
And married by Ebenr Jenkins Esq June 5th 1800

The intention of marriage between Thomas Backus & Rebecca Couch both of Lee made public May 1800   Married Octr 30 1800 by Revd A.Hyde

The intention of marriage between Philip Packard of Stockbridge and Rachel Gifford of Lee, made public Aug. 11th 1800
Married Septr 1 1800 by Revd Hyde

The intention of marriage between Job Childs of Lee & Nabby Hamblin of Lenox made public Aug. 17th 1800 +

The intention of marriage between Asael Stanton & Polly Ball ‡ both of Lee made public Septr 7th 1800   Married Octr 6th 1800 by Revd Alvan Hyde

The intention of marriage between Ebenr Porter & Eunice Yale both[of] Lee made public Septr 14th 1800   Married Jany 8th 1800 [1801] by Revd Alvan Hyde

† This intention also entered (same date) on Lenox T. R., Book 1 (original), p. 304.
‡ See p. 108.

The intention of marriage between Amasa Porter & Betsey Winegar
both of Lee made public Septr 14th 1800 Married Octr 30—1800 by A Hyde

The intention of marriage between Job Childs & Rhodah Hatch both of
Lee made public Septr 28th 1800   Married Octr 30 1800 by Rev A Hyde

The intention of marriage between James Nye & Thankful Crocker both
of Lee, made public Octr 12th 1800   Married Jany 23—1801 by Rev. A Hyde

The intention of marriage between Edward Hatch of Lee & Lucy Taylor Lenox made public Octr 12th 1800 ‡

The intention of marriage between James Whiton & Deborah Bassett
both of Lee made public Novr 9th 1800   Married Decr 18 1800 by Rev. A
Hyde

The intention of marriage between Matthew Vandusen of Lee & Betsey
Brayman of Tyringham, made public Novr 9th 1800

The intention of marriage between Revd Jabez Chadwick of Salem &
Sally Stewart of Lee, made Public Decr 1800)
Married Jany 8t[h] 1801 by Revd Alvan Hyde —

[Among the entries in 1803, is the following:]

This may certify that the intention of marriage between John Remmele
& Hannah Barlow both of Lee [was] made public Feby 16, 1796 married
by Revd Alvan Hyde April 19th 1796

‡ This intention is also in the Lenox Records (same date), and the marriage recorded
as follows: "1801, Jany 1st Edward Hatch of Lee to Lucy Taylor of Lenox."

Note—From the appearance of the Records, it would seem that the publishments and
marriages were not always promptly recorded, but were allowed to accumulate and
entered when convenient.   Thus several of Nathan Dillingham's publishments were
recorded by the succeeding clerk, Daniel Wilcox.   The entries also, are not always
given chronologically, and there are several entered twice.   The small number
of entries between 1780 and 1790 can only be explained on the presumption that they
are not all given.
    The marriages of several Lee people have been found on the records of other towns,
and will be given in the appendix.

Records of Births.

Note:—The following family birth records, which in the original are scattered over many pages without order, are arranged alphabetically for convenience of consultation.——All births recorded prior to January 1, 1801, are given, and every record commenced, given in full, except those of Ransom and Polly Hinman, and Reuben and Susanah Carey - no children being born to them until after the above date.

In some of these family records, all the births seem to have been recorded at the same time; in others after one or more had been recorded, space was left, which in some cases remains blank, but in some, more space, as the years passed was required, and the record was continued on another page.

Children of Seth Abbot Jr & Irene his wife

Cynthia born Septr 23, 1797

Children of Benjamin Adams & Sarah his wife

James T. born July 7th 1797.

Joseph Freeman Austin, son of James and Achsah Austin, born May 3d 1790 ——
Zafne Austin born Feb. 18th 1792 Died Aug. 26, 1793
An infant born May 4. 1798 Died May 4, 1798
John   Novr 9 1799

Children of Ichabud Backus & Deliverence his wife

Deborah born	Jany 29 — 1779	Simeon	Apl 16	1786
Joshua born	Apl 16 — 1781	Cornelius	Octr 8th	1788
Job,	Feby 10 — 1784	David	March 31 —	1791

Deliverence his wife died Novr 13th 1793

Children of Walley Backus, & Grace his wife.

Alma Gager, born Octr 25th 1794.	Elizabath born Octr 24	—	1807
Azel Huntington, Jany 26th 1797.	Walley	— Dec 23	-	1809
Remember Toby, July 8th 1799.	Leander	— June 10,	1812
Walley, Augt 4th 1801. Died	Jane E	March 19,	1814
Mathew Vandusen,Jany 15th 1804.	George Allen	Feby 27	1817.

A Son, born May 6th 1806, & died May 7th

Children of Thomas Bailey, & Esther his wife.

Smith born in Haddam, Connecticut Novr 31 1789.

Wealthy	May 13th 1792.	David	April 21 1801.
Orren	July 21st 1794.	Oliver	Octr 30th 1803.
Thomas born	May 28th 1797.		

Children of David Baker & Silvina his wife

Sally	born	Septr	10th	1784	
Lydia	—	March	5th	1786	
Lemuel	—	July	8th	1788	
Silvina	—	Octr	20th	1790	
David	—	Septr	1st	1793	
Samuel Crocker	born	May	9th	1796	
John	—	Feb.	16	1799	
Avis	born	Septr	2d	1801	Died the same day
An infant	born	Novr	14th	1802	& died Novr 15th 1802
Ebenr		Apl	3d	1804	Died Apl 4th 1804
Nancy	Born	Feby .	22,	1806	
Avis Crocker		August	16th	1808	

Children of Nathan & Ruhamah Ball

Nathan	Born	Feby	23	1768	– in Stockbridge	
Lydia	"	June	6th	1769	Do	
Polly	"	March	16th	1772	Do	
Sarah	"	April	25th	1773	Do	— Died
Elizabeth	"	Jany	21st	1775	Do	
Martha	"	May	13th	1776	— Lee	
John	"	July	25th	1777	"	
Anna	"	Decr	14th	1778	"	
James	"	Octobr	18th	1781	"	
Samuel	"	Augt	20th	1783	"	
Isaac	"	July	1st	1786	"	
Joseph	"	April	30th	1787	"	
Sally	"	Octobr	31st	1788	"	

Children of Nathan Ball, & Fear his wife.

Lucy	born	Oct⟨r⟩ 17th 1798.	Rhoda	born	Jan⟨y⟩ 6th 1807.
Nancy	—	July 20th 1800.	William	—	July 20, 1809
Amanda	—	Sept⟨r⟩ 19th 1802.	Rhode	—	May 1, 1812
Nathan	—	Aug⟨st⟩ 31st 1804.	Harriot	—	March, 1814

Children of Lot Barden, & Lucinda his wife.

Sally,	born	June 2d 1795.	Jerusha,	born	April 8th 1803.
Deborah,	—	Feby 17th 1797.	Asa,	—	May 16th 1805.
Betsey,		Feby 27th 1799.	Isaac	—	July 10 1807.
Elijah,		May 29th 1801.			

Lydia R. Barlow, Daughter of Peleg & Esther Barlow, born Feb. 5th 1798.

Children of Ancel Bassett & Hannah his wife.

an Infant born May 6, 1797 Died May 26—1797
Ephraim Dimmuck born Nov⟨r⟩ 16th 1798.
Cynthia born Jan⟨y⟩ 28th 1802
Semantha born July 24 18.5
Nancy Born August 31st 1807 ——
Marietta " Octobr 17th 1810 ——

Children of Reuben Barlow and Nabby his wife

An infant born —— 15th 1793 and Died March 16th 1793 —
An infant born Sept⟨r⟩ 17th 1796 and died the same day —
Joseph Warren born June 8th 1798
Samuel Born April 13th 1802

Children of Cornelius Bassett & Remember his wife

Elisha	born	Jan⟨y⟩ 22 1782.—
John	—	Jan⟨y⟩ 3 - 1784
Nathan		June 29 1785
a n infant		July 13–1791 Died July 1791
Remember Nye		May 6—1793
Experience		March 6-1796
Rachel		July 25th 1799

Children of Cornelius Bassett Jr and Abigail his wife

Nancy born Monday March 1 - 1784 & died of the Small Pox March 19th 1785
     Nancy   born Tuesday April 24 1786
     Lemuel born Friday 18th April 1788
     Lydia born Wednesday June 9th 1790
     Thomas born Sabbath April 14th 1793
Harriet born - Sabbath January 10th 1796 Died Jany 19th 1798
     Cornelius born   Aug. 31st 1799.

———

Children of Nathanl Bassett & Bethiah his Wife

Deborah Webb Bassett	born	August	18th	1782
Hannah	—	—	May	30th	1784
John Smith	—	March	29th	1787. Died Septr 12th 1806.
Nabby	—	—	— Decr	14	1789
Polly	—	—	— Feby	26	1792
Nathaniel	—	—	— June	12	1794
Isaac	—	—	— Jany	18 - 1797
Joseph	—	—	— Aug — 7 — 1799 Died Aug. 10 1800
Joseph born	—	—	— March 27 - 1801 —
Harriet	—	—	— Septr 12th 1803 —

———

Children of Aron Benedict and Marah his wife ——

Esther born May 1 - 1778 Died May — 1778
Eunice   July 11 - 1779 Died July 13 1779
Clarissa born August 7 - 1780   Aron Aug. 18-1786
Stephen   Novr 9 - 1782   Desire Novr 18-1788
Lucinda   Aug 7 - 1784   Nathn July 1 1790 Died July 3-1794
     Marah his wife died July 11-1790 —
     Married Betsy Randal 1791
     Betsey born Jany 21-1792   Eunice Decr 4 - 1793
     Molley   Jan 21-1792   Huldah Octr 11 - 1795

———

Children of George Bennett and Betsey his wife
Henry born June 21 - 1788
Betsey born Apl 7th 1790 died Septr 8 - 1790
     Prudence born March 3 - 1792   Betsey born March 7 - 1796

———

Children of Joseph Brace & Mary his Wife
     Harry born July 22, 1795   Caroline Augt 12 1801
     Charles   April 11, 1799   Elisha Nov 9, 1803

† Last figure omitted.

Children of Asael I. Bradley & Abigail his wife
Noah Roger born Octr 29 - 1797

Children of Eli Bradley & Phebe his wife

Philo born	Octr 2 - 1783	Sall	Octr 6 - 1793
Celia	Septr 16- 1785	William	Feb. 25 - 1796
Anne	Octr 7 - 1787	Eli, born July 31st 1798	
Polly	June 19th 1789	Phebe, born July 13th 1803.	
Josiah	July 31 - 1791		

Colonel Jared Bradley born Aug. 25 - 1760
Charity his first wife born March - 4 1759
Their Children as follows

Esther born Tuesday July 23-1782 Abigail born Thursday January 26-1786
Stephen - Thursday March 25-1784 Rhoda - Friday March 21-1788
Charity his wife Died July 31-1790
Married Phebe Munson June 8 1791
and born February 7-1767
Charity born Friday March 23 - 1792
Rachel born Monday Novr 25 - 1793
Thomas Ensine Munson born April 9 - 1796

Jared, born Octr 3 1798	Anson born Apl 15, 1805
Charity, born Nov. 22d 1800	Mary — Sept 5, 1807
Harriot — Decr 24th 1802	Hannah E. Jan 12, 1811

Children of Jesse Bradley Jr and Lucy his wife

An infant born Jany 27th 1791 and Dead	Lucy born Aug. 13 1799
Betsey born Feb. 26, 1792	Jesse born Aug. 3d 1802.
Amanda born Octr 26 - 1794	Erastus born July 6th 1806.
Lydia born Decr 2 - 1796	Amanday, born April 27, 1815

Children of Joseph Bradley and Eunice his wife
An infant born May 23, 1789 and Died immediately

Senath	— Sepr 14 - 1791.	Eunice born Novr 16 - 1794
Joel	— March 22 - 1793	Pamelia — July 25th 1798 —

Children of Seth Burden & Bethiah his wife.

Betsey, born Dec‡ 1ˢᵗ 1791. Died Jan. 2ᵈ 1797.

David,	—	Sept. 27th 1793.	William born	Dec‡ 9th 1805.
Thomas	—	June 10th 1796.	—	Dec‡ 20ͭh 1806.
Thankful	—	Aug‡ 27th 1798.	Simeon —	Aug‡ 11 - 1807
Bethiah	—	June 9th 1800.	Hannah —	Sep‡ 11 - 1809
Seth		Aug‡ 10th 1802.	Ezra —	Sep‡ 15 - 1812

[A part'al, duplicate list is also given on another page of the Records, as the children of Seth Barden and Bethiah his wife.]

Reuben Carey   born Feb 2ⁿ‡ 1777
Wife Susanah   " Oct‡ 4, 1783

[No child born until 1835.]

Children of Abiathar Chadwick and Desire his wife

Fear born	Oct‡ 19th 1778	Mary born	July 21ˢᵗ 1784
Heman —	June 11 — 1780	Archalaus -	June 30ͭh 1786
Joseph	Feb. 15 - 1782	Rhodema -	May 27—1788

Desire his wife died Aug—13—1790 —
Married Bathsheba Stewart Oct‡ 1791—

Charles born	June 19—1792.	Bathsheba July	25—1796 —
Desire —	Dec‡ 15--1793	Abiathar Octobr	30ͭh 1799 —

Children of Archalaus Chadwick and Sarah his wife

Thomas born monday March 3ᵈ   1777
Jabez born Saturday August 14th 1779
Elisabeth born thursday July 27th 1781
John born Monday Novr 15th 1782 And Died October 4th 1784 -
John born Monday August 23ᵈ 1784
Samuel born Saturday February 24th 1786 And Died August 29th 1787
Sarah born Saturday October 30th 1787
Samuel born Sabath August 24th 1789
Rhoda born   February 12th 1792
Ancel born Thursday November 21ˢᵗ 1793
Daniel born Monday August 22 1796

Children of George Chanter & Martha his wife

William born Oct‡ 27'h 1788 —

Children of Levi Chase and Temperence his wife

Polly   born   Decr 5 — 1777
Silence born July 31 — 1779
Levi   May 25 — 1781
Marcy   Jany 8th 1782   Died Feb. 5th 1782
Seth   March 13 - 1783   Died May — 1783
Thomas   June 1 — 1785
Nabby   Ap^l 17 1788
Betsey   Decr 2 — 1789 —
Tabitha   July 7 — 1791   Died July 27—1791 —

Children of Daniel Church & Hannah his wife

Rachel   born   July 26th 1770.
Daniel   June 8th 1772   Died May 10—1783
Levi   Aug. 14th 1775
Eli   Aug. 19th 1777
Danl   Septr 8 — 1783   Died Feb. 16 1784

Hannah the wife of Daniel Church Died April 15th 1784
Married Anne Bates Septr 20th 1785

Hannah born Aug. 7th 1787.   Anne   June 16th 1791

Children of Jesse Clark & Sarah his wife

Eli   born Septr 30 - 1779   John   Feb. 14th 1793
Cynthia   Septr 22 - 1782   Charles   July 1 — 1795
Jesse   Aug 21 - 1784   Alma   born October 3^d 1797
Sarah   Aug. 24 - 1786   Chauncy Fenner Decr 20th 1799
Mildred   Aug. 21 - 1788   Ruth   May 24th 1802-
Triphenia   Novr 5 - 1790

Children of Jonathan Clark, & Desire his wife.

Jonathan,   ⎫   Septr 20th 1784.
Joshua,   ⎪   April 11th 1786.
Abel Potter, ⎬ born in Charlestown, Rhode island. Octr 1st 1788.
Rebecca,   ⎪   Feb^r 16th 1790.
Amy,   ⎭   July 22^d 1793.

Samuel,   born Octr 14th 1795.   Sylvia,   born July 9th 1801.
Joseph Crocker,born Novr 21st 1797.   Alvan,   — Octr 3^d 1803.

Children of Archabald Collins and Rhoda his wife

Hannah born Novr 24th 1788

Children of Samuel Couch & Hannah his Wife

Marcus	born May 26, 1790		Hannah	born July 23, 1802
Phebe	— June 26, 1793		Ferriss	— Nov 14, 1806
Fhirza	— Feb 14, 1795 —			

Children of Stephen Couch & Polly his wife

John Morton born March 7—1794   Susanna   Aug 10—1797

Children of Elisha Crocker & Lucy his wife

David born Octr 27th 1775 —   William born June 18 1789
Zernah born January 18 1778   Electa Lewis May 16th 1791
Sophia born Novr 22—1779   John Dimmuck March 14 1793
Mira born Septr 17th 1781   Lucy born May 12 —1795.
Laura born March 18— 1784   Lucius, born April 16th 1798.
Elisha born Novr 11 1785   Zernah born Sept. 21st 1801.

Children of Jedediah Crocker and Sally his wife

Noah born Aug. 3-1783   Elizabeth Apl 16—1792
Jedediah Davis born May 30 1785   Polly May 2—1795
Sarah March 19-1787   Philna Aug 1798.
Samuel Apl 17—1790 .

Children of Joseph Crocker & Martha his wife

Sarah born March 16—1782   Asa June 19—1792
Benjn born 14—1784   Abigail Octr 1 - 1794
Chrysilda 18—1786   Joseph born Apl 1 1797
Betsey Clark Novr 18—1788   William born March 26—1800
Polley Apl 3—1790   Sabrina March 26 1803

Children of Joseph Crocker Jr and Polly his wife

Elizabeth Wormer born Septr 4-1790
Marcy Hamlin Decr 1 1791 Died Sept 7—1795 —
Temperence born Novr 10 1793 ——
Joseph born Decr 17—1795 Died July 24—1796 ——
Joseph Crocker Jr died Jany 8 1796 in the 30th Year of his age ——

Children of Josiah Crocker & Hannah his wife

Seth   born Jany 5—1796
Thomas   March 15—1797 Died April 6—1797
Betsey Crosby born Apl 3d 1798 Died Decr 23—1798
    Josiah born Septr 23d 1799.   Theressa born Febr 5th 1804.
    Betsey born March 3d 1801.   Thomas born March 23d 1805.
    —— born Jany 12th 1803   An infant died Feby 4 1804 †

Children of Abijah Crosby, & Caty his wife.

Abner, born Novr 4th 1795.   Charles, born Decr 11th 1801.
Lyman, — April 16th 1798.   Thomas — Decr 14th 1804.

Children of John Crosby Jr and Salome his wife

An infant born March 24 1793 Died Apl 21—1793
An infant born Apl 21—1795 Died May 1st 1795
Salome born July 23-1796.   Joseph born July 13, 1805
Horace born Aug. 12, 1799   Josiah — June 28, 1809
John,   Jan 31, 1801 —   Charles — July 4, 1811
Anna,   March 23, 1803

Children of Calvin Davis & Hannah his Wife

Joseph born Feb. 25th 1779.   Isaac born Septr 8th 1801.

Calvin Davis, Son of Isaac Davis, born March 5th 1778. —

Reuben Davis Son to John Davis born June 8th 1783

Children of Nathan Davis and Lucy his wife

Jedediah born May 2—1779 Died May 16—1779
Sarah   March 21—1780 Died Novr 1780
Lucy born Septr 11—1781   Isaac   Decr 30—1791
Hannah   Octr 30—1783   Bathsheba August 26—1794
Nathan   Feb. 16 1786   Hope   July 17—1796
Charita   August 18—1789 —   Marcy   July 1799

Children of Saml Davis & Priscilla his wife

Sally born August 16—1782 -   Saml born June 1790
Hope   March 1783 —   Priscilla Apl 1792
Parmele Jany 1785   Wait Novr 26—1794
Rebeca   May 15—1787   Lewis March 1797

† Feb. 7, in chl. rec.

Children of Solomon Davis and Martha his Wife

Sally Davis born May 24th 1783
Patty — Apl 26 1785
Bathsheba — June 27 — 1787
Oziel — Apl 2d 1789

Lucinda born Sepr 21 1791
Betsey Feb. 19—1794
Solomon born Aug. 25—1796

Children of Timothy Davis and Tabitha his wife born March 2d 1741 —

Mary	born	Falmouth	Novr 29th	1761
Thomas	born	Do	May 9th	1764
Anna Davis		Do	April 22d	1766
Rowland Davis		Do	Aug. 3	1770
Ephraim	born	Do	Octr 11 —	1772
Timothy	born	Do	Octr 21 —	1774 ——

Children of Stephen Dexter & Lydia his wife

Benjamin Backus born July 30—1795
Eveline born Jany 27 1798

Children of Nathan & Rebecca Dillingham born

Sarah Dillingham	born	Saty	Octr 11th	1783.
Abigail Dillingham	born	Saty	Feby 25th	1786
Rebecca Dillingham —		Friday	Feby 29th	1788.
William Henry Dillingham	Tuesday	Augt 3d		1790.
Lucy Dillingham	born	Saturday, July	14th	1792.
Nathan Dillingham			Octr 17th	1794.
John Dillingham		Thursday Feb.	16 —	1797
Charles — ——	born	Monday July	22	1799
Nancy,	born		April 26th	1802.
George Washington	born		Octr 26th	1804.
Bourn Green	Born		May 30th	1807

Children of Asahel Dodge and his wife, born as follows

Hanah, born January 12th 1776
Seymour, — April 29th 1778
Abraham — Septemr 29th 1780 -
Heman — Novr 7th 1782

Asahel born Novr 23d 1784
Sarah — March 18th 1787
Samuel — May 29th 1792

Children of Elisha Dodge & Betsey his wife

Harriot —	born	Aug. 13th 1799.
Almira	born	June 6th 1802.
Elisha	—	July 12th 1805.

Children of Henry & Hannah Donnelly ———

Eleazer Donnelly born Novr 9th 1788.
George Gardner Donnelly born Novr 13th 1791.

Children of Silas Easton and Rachel his wife

Polly born January 30th 1795 and Died February 15th 1795
Thomas Nye born Octr 20th 1796

Children of Paul Ewer & Marcy his wife

John born Septr 2—1783 --		Nabby		1791
Tilson	1785	Martha		1793
Polly	1787	Paul	March 28—1795 —	
Jane	June 7—1789			

Marcy his wife Died March 28—1795

Children of Abraham Finney & Huldah his wife

Ezra born August 23d 1795
an infant born Jany 17—1797   Died Jany 17—1797

Children of Ancel Finney & Polly his wife

Barnabas born July 23d 1798.
Benjamin Franklin born June 3d 1801 Died Septr 2d 1802 —
Leman Franklin born June 6th 1803 —   Mary born March 13th 1811.
Caleb Barnum born July 22d 1805.   Anselm Jr. November 2d 1814.
Amanda Manerva   June 26th 1807.

Children of Barnabas Finney & Deborah his wife

Ancel born Decr 25th 1773 —   Calvin   Feb. 7th 1777
Benjn   May 23—1775 —   Sylvanus Decr 15th 1778 —
Barnabas Finney died June 30—178   [Last figure omitted.]
Deborah Finney Married Nath! Tobey——Their Children
    Experience born Dec^r   28—1782
    Samuel   Oct^r   22—1784 —
    Marah   Septr 18—1786
    Cynthia   May   17—1792 —
    Barnabas   March 18 1795—Died Ap! 17—1795.

Children of Jonathan Finney and Sarah his wife

Polly   born Octr 19th 1789 Died Novr 1—1791
George   born Ap!   2—1791   Phebe   Feb. 15—1794
Polly   July 2—1792   Selden   Septr 1—1795

Children of Alvan Foot & Sally his wife

Twins born Aug. 4th 1799 One died same day The other's name is
John William
Alvan, born   June 10th 1801.   Sarah — May 22, 1808 —
Elisha Percival, born, March 10th 1803.   Jonathan, Dec. 5, 1812 —
Marshal,   born, Nov. 28th 1805.   Harriot — April 3, 1815
                                      Huldah Jane Feby 7 1821

Children of Asael Foot and Anne his wife —

Sally born Ap! 2—1794   Amanda   —   — Jany 13th 1803—
Elizabeth Decr 25—1795 — Asahel & Anne twins born Decr 16th 1804
Lyman   July 9th 1798   Lydia   —   Sepr 13, 1807—
Charles May 12th 1800)

Children of David Foot & Betsey his wife

Betsey   born   June 23—1786 —
Thomas   May 21 1788
Silas   Aug. 18—1791
David   July 11 1792—Died Octr 13—1792
Deliverence   May 3 1794   Temperance, born Nov. 7th 1800.
Laovisa   Novr 29th 1796   Ransom,   Feb. 15th 1802.

Children of Elisha Foot & Dille his wife & born Apr. 29—1785

Chandser	born Aug. 19—1797	Sophia	— July 13th 1807
Amelia	born Feby 1st 1799	Elisha	—— Augt 1, 1809
Justus Battle	Jany 25th 1801	Delia	born at Lenox Apl 5, 1814.
Ransom Hinman April 13th1803		Geo. Franklin born at albany	
Henrietta	Jany 19th 1805		March 13 1817

Children of Fenner Foot and Sarah his wife

Lucinda born Septr 8th 1779		Erastus born Septr 4 1792	
Calvin	born Decr 15—1781	Fenner	born Octr 10 1794
Daniel	born Feb. 17—1784	Sena	born Octr 18th 1796
Olive	born Feb. 2—1786	Cyrus	born June 18th 1800.
Jerusha born Octr 20—1789			

Children of Jonathan Foot Jr an[d] Deliverence

Elisha born	Jany 22 1775 —		
Alvan	May 29—1777		
Jerusha	May 22—1780 and died Decr 9—1780 ——		
Jerusha	Decr 23—1781	John May 7—1791 Died Octr 25—1791	
Sylvanus	Apl 12—1785	William Aug-24—1793—& Died Octr 1793	
Jonathan	Feb. 11—1788 —		

Children of Lovisa Foot

Melinda born July 22 1789 — Parthenia Octr 12, 1790

Children of Elisha Freeman and Elizabeth his wife

Benjamin born Jany 21—1775			
Thomas	June 27 1777 and Died June 28 1780		
Betsey	March 27—1779	Thomas born July 28—1786	
Elisha	Septr 4—1781	Lydia	Novr 10—1788
Fanny	March 14—1784	Charles	March 16 1793

Children of Wm Freeman & Jerusha his wife

Alva Freeman born October 12th 1791
Sally — born Novr 10th 1793
John Percival born February 23— 1797
Betsey — born February 23 1797 Died March 7—1797
Betsey — born July 18th 1799.

Children of Varmun Gardner & Mehitable his wife

Sabrina, born Sepr 28, 1795 —		Elisha — born Nov 28, 1803–
Ira, born Augt 4, 1797 —		Benjamin born Dec 5, 1809
Lophina, born Augt 20, 1799 —		Mehitable born March 10, 1812
James, born Dec 1, 1801 —		Caroline, born May 17, 1814

Children of James Gifford & Sarah his wife

Eunice born Aug. 27th 1792	Charles Peck born Aug 30, 1805
James born March 10th 1798	

Children of Jesse and Ruth Gifford

Caty born	March 3—1775	Thos born	Apl 17—1785
Betsey	Aug. 20th 1777	Lydia	June 10—1787 —
Celia	May 22—1779	Nabby	Apl 11—1789 —
Abraham	Jany 8th 1781	Ruth	Octr 18th 1792
Phebe	March 23—1783	Alvan	Jany 13th 1794

Children of John Gifford and Johannah his wife

Sylvanus born Septr 10th 1781 —		John born May 31—1785
Sylvia May 18 — 1783		Jeneverah born Decr 23—1787
Erastus Decr 29—1791—Died Jany 5—1792			
Jesse born Feb - 19—1793 Died June 29 —1794			
Lewis Apl 7—1795 Died Apl 11—1795			
Sally born Jany 31 1797		Lewis born May 19, 1800

Children of Elisha Grant & Marah his wife

Elisha born	Decr 29—1774	
Ruth	August 22--1776	
Esther	Octr 14—1778	
Prudence	Decr 7—1780	
Jared	Septr 6—1782	Died May 15 1785
David born	June 4—1784 --	
Thankful	May 12—1786	
Orris	Octr 16—1788	
Eunice	Apl 17—1791	Died March 19—1794
Polly born	Octr 23 —1793	Died Novr 10—1795 —
Isaac born	Aug. 29, 1797	

Children of Jonathan Graves & Anne his wife

Archalaus	born Septr 10th 1783	
Joseph	Novr 5—1785	
Jonathan	Apl 17—1788	
Anne	Apl 17—1788	
Lester	Decr 21 1790	
John	Decr 21 1790	Died Decr 22—1790
Rebeca	Aug. 21—1793	Died Aug. 20—1795 —
Rebeca	Octr 27—1796	

Alvan & Alma—Twins born Feb. 23d 1799

Children of John Green & Martha his wife

Philo born Decr 14 1791	Shubel born Feby 17th 1799.
William born Jany 16—1794	Abisha — Feb. 26th 1801.
Daniel born Novr 3—1795	Sally born Feby 24 1803
Jerusha born Apl 17—1797	Huldah May 12th 1805.

Children of Abraham Hall & Rachel his wife

Lydia born Jany 6th 1799	Harriot — Feb 27, 1807
John " June 15 1801	Albert — Feb 1, 1809
Alma born March 25th 1803.	

Children of Abraham Hall & Second Rachel his wife

Linus P — born Sepr 23d 1810
Rachel —— March 28, 1812 —
Luther Chaffee May 11, 1816

Children of Moses Hall, & Relief his wife.

Charles, born Septr 12th 1798.	Reuben)
Nancy. - April 14th 1800.	Relief) Twins, born Augt 9th 1804.
Lucy, — May 29th 1802.	

Children of Cornelius Hamlin and Mercy his wife

Job born April 21—1795 —
William Finney June 21—1796—Died Octr 23—1797

William	Feb. 11 1799	Marcy,	Nov 22, 1809.
Stephen	June 21, 1802.	Mary —	Jan 20, 1811.
Lucy F.	April 11, 1804	Job —	Jan 15, 1813
Hannah,	June 12, 1806.		

Children of David Hamlin and Sally his wife

Nabby born Aug. 4—1795	Nathaniel	————
Maria, June 23, 1797.	Benjamin Augt 8. 1809	
David July 23, 1802.		

Children of Widow Anne Handy

Obed Handy born Octr 16 1777   Darius Carpenter born May 18–1790
Ebenr Handy born May 21—1779   Orsiah Hoose   — June 19 1793.
Elizabeth Handy - Apl 15—1784

Children of Wait Hatch & Marah his wife

ʰ Rebeca born ——- 1756 Died May 1—1788
Edward born June 11ʰ 1776 —

Children of Moses Hill & Polly his wife

Lucy born Feb. 9—1783	Ira Decr 1787
Justus born Feb. 9th 1785	Silas Aug. 1789
Moses born June 1786	Sally Jany 1795
Polly Septr 1787	Harvey March 16.1797

Children of Benjamin Hinckley & Puella Goodspeed his wife

Electa Hinckley Born   Thomas Goodspeed Born
Warren Hinckley Born April 24. 1795
Charles Hinckley ——- Oct 22 1800
Luther Thacher Hinckley

Children of Heman Hinkley and Lydia his wife

Zenas born June 12–1779	Edmund Apl 27—1789
Polly born Apl 26—1781	Carolina Novr 1—1791
Lucretia Octr 13—1783	Heman August 22—1793
Silas Octr 1—1785	Benjamin
Lydia March — 1787 —	

Children of Joseph Hinkley, & Polly his wife

Nabby	born April 14th 1796.	Barnabas A —	March 23, 1808
Sally	— July 5th 1799.	Luman —	June 12, 1810
Edmund	— Aug! 29th 1800.	Mary —	June 10, 1812
Hudson	— Aug. 12th 1803.	Bradford	Feb. 26, 1817
Content Lovel -	July 3d 1805.	Bathsheba	March 22, 1823

Children of Zina Hinkley, & Elizabeth his wife.

Priscilla born Oct! 28th 1799.
Eliza — Oct! 2d 1802. Died Oct! 17th 1806.
Alvira — Sept! 12th 1804.
William · Aug! 2d 1806.

Ransom Hinman Born May 14th 1785 —
Polly Battle his Wife " June 5th 1785—in Tyringham
[No child born until 1805.]

Children of Abraham Howk & Esther his wife

Hannah born Oct! 24—1793—
Roxe June 1795 — Died Jany 3d 1799

Children of Andrew Howk & Betsey his wife

An infant born Dec! 20th 1799 Died Dec! 21st 1799

Children of Isaac Howk & Fiche his wife

Richard	born Ap! 1- 1787 —	Fiche born	April 16 — 1795 —
Caty	Sept! 25—1788 —	Alonson. born Sept! 15, 1799 —
John	March 15 1791	Electa, born, Oct. 17, 1801
Isaac	July 23, 1793 —		

Isaac Howk Sen. Died Jany 29th 1805

Children of John Howk and Caty his wife

David	born March 20—1786 —	Mariah born	Dec! 2—1794
Clarry	March 19th 1788	Eliza,	Oct. 14, 1797 —
John	Feb. 7—1790	William,	Jan 19, 1802 —
Caty Hollembeck Jany 25 1793 —		Alburt,	June 28, 1806

Children of John Hulett & Sarah his wife --

Achsah   May 5—1784 —
Betsey   Aug -5—1786 —
John   Aug 25—1788 and Died Oct? 15—1796
Wealthy   May 19th 1795 + — Died Feb. 8th 1794.
Sally   Feb. 21 1793 and Died June 28—1793
Westley   Aug! 15—1794 —
John   Oct? 13—1796

Sarah his wife died Jany 21—1797 —

Children of John Hulet & Sarah his wife ‡ ——

Isaac	born	June 22. 1792++	Teressa born Feb 26. 1805
Sally	——	Jan 2. 1799	Betsey	April 7. 1811
Abijah	——	Aug! 24, 1801	Samuel	Feb. 3, 1814
Fletcher	——	April 6, 1803		

Children of Sam! Hulett and Susanna his wife

Chauncy born March 14th 1790 --   Orren born May 17—1796
Electa   May 3d 1793

Children of Sylvanus Hulett and Mary his wife

Sally born Oct? 29th 1787.   Charlott born Nov? 7—179‡‡
Charles born March 3—1790 —   Rhoda born June 8th 1795

Children of Rev,d Alvan Hyde and Lucy his wife

Alvan born June 18th 1794   William born Aug! 16th 1806.
Charles Backus March 24th 1796   Edward born Sept 15th 1808
Harriot born March 19— 1798   Chauncey Thompson Sept 25th 1810
Stephen born March 24th 1800   Theodore born Aug! 5, 1812
Joseph born Sep! 3d 1802   Alexander Hyde Sept 25 1814
Lucy born June 3 1804

‡ Date of birth erroneous—The date of death corresponds,within a day, of that given by Dr. Hyde.

‡ Presumably this name should be Hannah—see page 140 for intention of marriage between John Hulett and Hannah Walker of Tyringham—proof of the marriage, however, cannot be given, for the marriage records of that town are wanting for this period.

++ Date printed as recorded.

‡‡ Last figure obliterated —name as recorded.

Children of Calvin Ingersoll and Lydia his wife ——

Electa	born	May 1— 1790	Cyrus	—	Septr	2, 1802
Vashti		Jany 14th 1792	— Lydia	—	Septr	1, 1804
Philo		Decr 2—1793	David Sanford	Oct.	23, 1806
Leml †		Jany 24—1796	— Edward M	— July	23, 1809
Horace,		June 23, 1798	Calvin	—	Feb.	5, 1812 —
Erastus		June 17, 1800				

———

Children of David Ingersoll and Sarah his wife ——

Erastus	born	Novr 9—1782	David	March 3—1795
Lucinda	born	June 2d 1784 —	Sarah	March 3—1795
Theodore		April 26—1786 —	Elizabeth	June 21—1797
Lucretia		Feb. 9, 1788	Lucy	June 6 1799—
Moses		February 15—1790 —	William & Alvan	†
Sophia		March — 1792 —	Elihu Parsons	

[The last three names appear to have been written long after the others.]

———

Children of Elijah Ingersoll & Polly his wife

Clarissa	born	May 24th 1787	Isaac	—— 1797
Barhsheba	—	Apl 14th 1789	Elisha	Jany 7th 1799
Nathan	—	Jany 8— 1791	Lucinda	—— 1802
Laban	—	Feby 5th 1793	George Washington	1804
Levi	—	March 10—1795 —		

———

Children of Jared Ingersoll and Elizabeth his wife

Ebenr Kniblow	born June 29—1784	Elizabeth	June	1795
Polly	June 5—1785	Rhoda	May 8 1797
Lois	Jany 29—1787	Ashur	born Nov 5, 1799
John	Septr 23—1788	Stephen J. "	Nov 6, 1801
David	June 10—1790	Phadime "	Oct. 24, 1803
Merit	March 16—1792	Milton "	Jan. 22, 1806
Reuben	Septr 26—1793	Jared "	July 30. 1808.

† See p. 108.

Children of Moses Ingersoll and Eunice his wife

Elener	born	March 11—1771	John Calvin	Ap¹	13—1780
Anne	born	March 13—1776	B'lley born	Ap¹	10th 1782
Luther	born	Jany 8—1778	Betsey born	Ap¹	10—1782

Eunice his wife died Novr 19th 1785 in the 50th year of her age ——

Children of Moses Ingersoll & Se[c]ond Prudence his Wife ——

Moses born May 27, 1797   Eunice born Sepr 13, 1798

Children of William Ingersoll Jr and Marcy his wife

Lydia	born	Novr 10th 1783	Joseph	Decr	22—1796—
Seth Crocker	born	May 1— 1785	James	May	7th 1799
William	born	March 21 1787	Marshal	Jan	29, 1802.
Celia		Jany 21— 1790	Charles	May	2, 1804.
Sarah		June 21— 1792	Harriot	Jan	21—1807
Thomas		Novr 2— 1794 —			

Children of Ebenezer Jenkins Junr & Lydia his wife.

Henry Willm	born	Aug. 17th 1793.	Lydia,	born	Sept. 3¹ 1800.
Nathan,	born	Feby 11th 1795.	Elizabeth,	born	July 1st 1802.
Josiah,	born	Nov. 9th 1796.	Warren,	born	April 12th 1804.
Ebenezer,	born	Sept. 12th 1798.	Marshal,	born	Aug. 15th 1806.

Children of Saml Jones and Remember his wife

Anne born   June 30 1793   Caroline born April 9th 1797

Deborah Smith born August 11—1795   Saml born May - 1799

Children of John Keep and Elizabeth his wife

Olive born July 30—1789   James   Septr 30 1792

Abbe   Jany 18 1791   Jabez   Feb. 11 1794

Elizabeth his wife Died Feb. 20 1796   Married Abigail Lenester

Lenester born Sep. 6—1797

Children of Arnold Lamphier & Anne his wife

Lois	(Windham)	Nov 26, 1796
Joseph (Wt Greenwich R. I.)		Oct 7, 1797
Lorticus	(Springfield)	Apl 13, 1799
Lyman	do	Feb 6 1801
Arnold	(Mansfield)	May 18 1803
Zalmon	(Washington)	Aug 18 1805
Anne	(Hinsdale)	Oct 27, 1807
Lena	(do)	Apr 8, 1810
Angelina Matilda (Saratoga)		March 22, 1812
Else	(Grafton N. Y.)	Feb. 18, 1816
Moses	———	——— 1818 died
Charles Bishop Moses (Lee)		Feb. 22, 1822

Children of Zacheus Maltby and Ruhamah his wife

Ezra Burchard born April 1—1798 —   Mercy born Feby 9th 1800

Betsey Mansfield born Jany 27--1772

Children of Reuben Marsh & Lydia his Wife

Alpheus born	Septr 27, 1792	William	— July 1, 1796
Triphena —	March 2, 1794	Amasa	— April 24, 1800

Children of Thomas Miller & Annis his wife

Daniel Gain Miller born Septr 23d 1796

Children of John Nye and Lois his wife

Stephen	born	Aug. 22—1780	Died Novr 10—1780
Esther		Novr 1—1781	Died Decr 1—1781
Hannah	born	Novr 17—1782	
John		Jany 19—1785	
Ira		———22—1787	Died May 22—1787
Ira		Apl 10—1788	
Esther		Decr 19—1790	
Lois		Feb. 22—1793	
Charles		Jany 6—1796	Died March 6—1796

Children of Levi Nye and Sarah his wife

Joshua	born	August 24th 1767	Levi	May 6th 1777
Benjamin		February 9th 1769	Sally	July 28 1780
Marah and Rachel		Septr 1 1772		
Thomas		Aug — 26—1774	Thomas Died	

Children of Seth Nye and Amey his wife

Elisha	born	Septr 23—1782	Betsey	born	Septr 13—1791
Jerod	born	Septr 5—1785	Joshua	born	Septr 26 1795
Caleb	born	Novr 24 1787	Sally	born	Novr 23—1797
Thankful	born	Aug. 26—1789			

Children of George Parker & Remember his wife.

Hannah	born	March 18th 1780	Mahala		Aug. 17, 1791
Rebecca		Aug. 31— 1782	Benjn		Jany 1795
Remember		Aug. 21 1784	Susana		May 21, 1797
Nathan		Decr 29, 1789			

Children of Salmon Peck & Anne his wife

Olive	born	Jany 7th 1793	Moses Ingersol born —
Hiram	born	Octr 5th 1797.	

Children of Jacob Penoyer and Alice his wife

Sally born Jany 19th 1795 - . — -   Marcy born Aug. 10th 1797

John Percival Born	November	6th 1754 at Sandwich
Ruth Percival Born	January	9th 1759 at Falmouth
Betsy Percival Born	October	20th 1777
Lydia Percival Born	february	12th 1779
John Percival Jur Born	April	25th 1781
Ruth Percival Born	April	25th 1783
Samuel Percival Born	August	29th 1785
James Percival Born	June	5th 1788
Mont Gomery Percival Born	Septr	25 h 1790
Hannah Gates Percival born	Jany	12 1793
Content	born Feb	28	1796
Nabby —	born Feb		1798

Children of Abm Perry and Temperence his wife

S[illegible] born	Apl 3—1789 — Died Apl 18—1789 —
Polly born	Apl 11—1790
Arthur born	Jany 27—1792
Diadama	Decr 9th 1793
Abram born	Decr 30 1797
Lyman	Jany 5th 1801 Died March 9th 1802.
Tempey born	Novr 4th 1803

Wm. Perry's children, p. 34

———

Sylvanus Phinney born Dec. 15. 1778
Lucy (formerly Kingsley of Becket,) his wife March 12, 1781
[No child born until 1803—This record found after the note on page 12 was printed.]

———

Children of Reuben Pixley Jr and Polly his wife
Reuben born Tuesday Octr 6th 1795

———

Children of Oliver Pool & Lucy his wife
Orrin born Aug. 23d 1797.   Lucy born May 1st 1800

———

Children of Levi G. Porter and   his wife

Huldah born	Feb. 28th 1786 and died March 13—1794
Philander	Feb. 29— 1788
Horace —	June 15— 1790
Rhoda —	Apl 20— 1792 and died June 5—1795
Levi Goodwin	Apl 10— 1794
Abel	Apl 15— 1796 ——

———

Children of Samuel Porter & Prudence his wife

Ebenezer born	Octr 8th 1776
Samuel	July 12— 1779 Died Feb. 20th 1784
Mary	Septr 17th 1781
Grace	Jany 2— 1784
Abigail	Octr 5th 1786
Laura	May 7th 1789
Lydia	July 25 1791
Kimbal	Novr 26— 1795 And died March 7th 1796

Joel Ducann's children, p. 34.

Children of John Reed & Elizabeth his wife ——

Amanda born May 21—1795   Anne born Decr 24th 1797
Fear   born May 26—1796   Paulina born June 24th 1799

Children of John Remmele & Hannah his Wife

Lydia born Sepr 3, 1797   Curtis)
Hannah — Feb 20, 1800   Calista) twins Sepr 22d 1806
John M — June 13, 1802

Children of Simeon Reynolds, & Zeruah his wife

Cyrus Almond, born	——	June 11th 1786.
Polly Asenath, born	——	March 23d 1791.
Edward, born	——	Sept 21st 1793.
Rachel, born in Benson Vermont,		April 8th 1800.
Lucy, born		Decr 1st 1803.
David, born		Aug. 31st 1806.
Simeon Jun		Jany 13 1809

Children of Amos Roberts & Susanna his wife ——

William	born	Novr	21— 1778 —		
Deborah	born	May	11th 1780		
Dorse	born	March	22— 1782, and died Octr 17th 1783		
Timothy	born	June	11— 1784 —	Susanna	Decr 11th 1793-
Amos		March	8th 1786	Sheirman	Apl 24th 1785 +
Anne	——	Apl	11th 1788 —	Elijah born June 18 1799.	
Dorse		June	28th 1790 —		

Children of Levi Robinson & Elizabeth his wife

Amos Benton	born Octr 9—1784‡ —	Polly	Feb.	18—1790
Sally	Novr 21- 1784‡	Fanny	August	9—1794
Betsey	July 26 1786	Amanda	Jany	31—1796

Children of Ephraim Sheldon & Lydia his wife

Lydia born May 6th 1795

† Doubtless intended for 1795.
‡ Dates printed as recorded.

Children of Benj⁹ Smith and Sarah his wife

Lydia	born	Septr	14—1777	Matthias born Feb.	10th 1786
Meribah —		Octr	24 1779	Sarah born	Feb.	21 —1788
Benj⁹		Novr	1—1781	Assenath	March 27 1793
William		Octr	8—1783		

Children of Ebenr Squire & Adrye his wife

Sally born Septr 18th 1781   Daniel born March 5—1784

Children of John Starnes and Lucy his wife ——

Polly	born	March	16 1780	
Sally	—	July	22—1781	
John	—	March	29—1783	
Abijah	.—	Octr	22 1784	Abijah Died 1786
Fanny	—	August	26—1786	
Thomas		July	5 1788	Died July 14—1799
Abijah	born	June	27 89	
Betsey	—	June	3—1790	Betsey Died Octr 5th 1799.
James	—	Octr	4—1792	
Bulah	—	Novr	2 · 1793	
Danl	—	Septr	29—1795	

Children of Benj⁹ Stevens and Sarah his wife

Susanna born Aug. 29—1785	Sally born	March 8—1791
Marcy	Aug 29—1787	Chauney	Jany 27—1793
Lucy	Feb 20 1789	Benj⁹	May 19 1795

Children of James Stevens and Lucretia his wife

An Infant born Decr 3—1792	Died Decr 3—1792
Richard Williams born	March 17th 1794 —
Norman Denison Born	March 18th 1798
Zar Banfford	"	March 25th 1800
Roxa Minerva	"	Decr 8th 1803
Lydia Millonia	"	March 7th 1807 —
Anna Williams	"	May 4th 1808

Children of Squire Stone & Rebecca his wife

Triphena	born June 20th 1790		Almes	born	Feb. 23, 1796
Harvey	March 9th 1792		Palmira		March 3 1798.
Zaphne	March 22 1794		William		Septr 13th 1799

Children of William Sturges & Salome his wife

Samuel born	June 2— 1796	John,	April 4, 1807.
Nabby born	May 24th 1798.	Persis,	May 4, 1809.
William	Aug. 1 1800	Ebenezer	Feb 7, 1812
Franklin born	Septr 4th 1802.	Eliza	July 4, 1814.
Sally	Septr 7th 1804.	Josiah	1816

Children of John Thatcher, & Parna his wife.

Luther Robinson born in Wareham Jany 15th 1791.
Hannah born in Wareham Septr 6th 1792.
Lucy born in Leicester June 1st 1796.
Thomas born Septr 9th 1798. Emily — April 4th 1806.
Sylvia — March 22d 1800. Harriot — March 7, 1808

Children of Timothy Thatcher, & Dorothy his wife.

Crocker, born Octr 9th 1800. Adah Ells — Feby 25th 1808 —
Charles Skinner, — May 5th 1802. Eliel — Feb—12— 1812
Betsey Freeman — Jany 23d 1803. Martha — Fely 5, 1815
Bulkley — March 22d 1806.

Children of Doct. Nathaniel Thayer, & Anne his wife.

William Austin, born in Woodbury, State of Connecticut, August 5th 1792.
Lucius Fowler, born in Durham, State of Connecticut, June 21st 1797.
Nancy Lucretia, born November 27th 1804.

Children of Elijah Thomas & Patience his wife

Patience born	Feb. 24—1780	Abraham	Aug. 11—1790
Nathan	Feb. 4—1783 —	Isaac	Aug. 11 1790
Asa	Novr 10—1785	Ezra	June 25 1794
		Rebeca	Septr 2—1796 —

Children of Dr Gideon Thompson & Olive his Wife

Rhoda born December 11th 1786	Chauncy	—	May 24	1790
Hezekiah Orton Novr 11th 1789	Olive	—	Aug. 1st 1793

Children of Samuel Tilley and Hannah his wife

Electa born July 16—1786
Marcy   June 21 1788   Died July 5—1789
Rhoda   Novr 13—1791   Lucy Apl 10 1794 —

For children of Nathaniel and Deborah Tobey, see page 53.

Children of Steph Tobey and Lydia his wife

Nathaniel born Septr 10th 1775 & died the 18th						
Remember born Apl 11 1777	Asael	born	Novr	21—1790
Celia	born Apl 10— 1780	Sarah	born	June	17 1793
Steph	born Decr 20— 1782	Mary	born	Aug.	14—1796
Lydia	born July 7 1785	An infant born March 12th 1799
Nathl	born Feb. 17 1788	Died same day

Children of Laurance Vandusen and Christeen his wife

Betsey   born   Octr 14 1790
Isaac   March 7—1793   Died Decr 4—1793
Andrew   Septr 8 1794   Christeen Van Deusen born May 27—1797

Richard Montgomery Walker, Son of Caleb & Huldah Walker, born Friday February 8th 1788——Huldah, Wife of Caleb Walker deceesed March 16th 1788
Caleb Walker died at Genesee in the Summer of 1790.——

Children of Henry Wansey & Chloe his wife

Betsey born Feb. 24—1783 —	Electa	Novr	24—1789
Reuben	May 10—1784	Esther	March	25—1791
John	Decr 28—1786	Lucretia	Apl	22—1793 —
Benjn	Apl 28--1788——	Jared	Apl	1—1795

Children of Daniel West and Elizabeth his wife

Elizabeth born	Feb. 28th 1776	Died Jany 23d 1785			
Zeruiah born	April 4th 1777	Elizabeth	March 18th 1788		
Thomas Tracy	Septr 21 1798 †	Orson	Jany 4— 1791		
Daniel born	Aug. 1, 1780.	Pelatiah	Feb. 26— 1793		
Lucy	May 19th 1782	Alvah	June 21— 1795		
Sally	Feb. 25— 1784	Eunice at Lenox	June 29th 1797		
Ira	May 24th 1786				

Children of Elijah West and Marah his wife

Jeduthan born	Novr 5, 1779	Erastus	Aug. 29—1783	
Orange	Aug. 5— 1781	Deborah	Septr 5—1785	
Parmelia	Aug. 27— 1787	Died March 12—1789		
Ashbel	May 10— 1789			
Wareham	Apl 7th 1791	Alpheus born	Novr 1—1795	
Sabara	June 28— 1793	Edna born	Decr 5—1797	

Mary West Daughter to Elisha West and Olive his Wife Born March the 4th 1772

Prudence West Daughter to Elisha West and Olive his Wife Born December the 9th AD: 1773

Ann West Daughter to Elisha West and Olive his Wife Born October the 31st AD: 1775

John Bruster West Son to Elisha West and Olive his Wife Born December the 11th AD: 1777

Children of Jonathan West & Elizabeth his wife

Miner born	Feb.	29— 1774				
David born	June	18th 1775	Died Octr 17—1777			
Lydia born	Octr	9th 1776	Died Octr 8—1777			
David	July	4— 1778	—			
An infant born	Jany	17th 1779	Died Jany 19—1779			
Jared	June	11— 1780				
an infant born	July	1781	— Died July —1781			
Betsey born	Aug.	5— 1782	Jonathan March 30—1786			
Laura	Feb.	11— 1784—	Thomas	Aug 24—1787		
Lydia	Decr	24— 1788	Died Decr 14—1790	—		
Lois born	Feb.	29— 1791	Alvan	May 29th 1793		
Lydia	Feb.	29— 1791	Susanna	Jany 15th 1795		

Jonathan West Died Septr 1795

† Evidently a mistake for 1778.

Children of Levi West and Bathsheba his wife who died Apl 20th 1805

Nabby   born   June   16— 1784
Nathaniel   Septr   13— 1785
Patty   August 13— 1787 Died April—1791 ——

Amasa   August 4th 1789 —
Patty   Novr   6— 1791   Anne   Feb. 29— 1796 —
Marcy   Novr   30— 1793 Mercy   June 18th 1798

———————

Children of Prince West and Hannah his wife —

Bathsheba born   Aug. 12— 1763.   Heman   born June 7th 1777.
Hannah   Jany 13th 1766   Amey   October 30th 1779 —
John   Feb. 15th 1770.   Philo   Feb. 16th 1782.
Sylvanus   July 23, 1772.   Ezekiel   May 2d 1784.
Christopher   Decr 14, 1774   Prince   Novr 1st 1786——

———————

Children of William Whitney and Sarah his wife born Aug. 13—1754

Nabby   born   Apl   10—1774   William   Jany 9—1782
Sarah   Apl   23—1776   Clarissa Septr 6—1785
Patty   Novr   6—1778   John   Jany 29—1788

Mary   June   26—1790   Died July 27—1790
Marah   Septr   27—1791
Richard   Feb.   10—1795   Died April 23—1796
Esther   Octr   5 1797

———————

Children of Joseph Whiton & Amanda his Wife

Semanthe   born   Augt   30, 1794   Edward V — June 2d 1805
Harriot   —   March   7, 1796   Eliza   — April 16, 1807
Amanda   —   Octr   10, 1797   Catharine — March 8, 1810
Joseph Lewis —   July   14, 1799   Agnes   — Augt 12, 1813
Daniel G   —   March   20, 1801

———————

Children of Daniel Willcox and Lydia his wife

Hudson born Monday October 12th 1795 ——
Electa born Saturday Apl 12   1800
John   born Sabbath Feby 21st   1802
Hudson Died May 28th Seven o Clock P. M. 1802

Children of Edward Willcox & Deborah his wife

Edward born Sept 14—1790   Sally   Feb. 22—1794 ——
Randal   Dec 9—1792

Peter Willcox born Killingsworth, June 6th 1735
Jerusha his wife born Coventry Dec —1738 and Died May 30th 1778
Their Children born as follows

Oziel born	Aug. 16—1759 and was Killed at Sheffield March 27th 1787		
Sarah born	Jany 30—1761	Jerusha born	March 22 1769
Daniel born	May 16th 1763	Ephraim Willcox Dec 24th 1773	
Peter born	July 12th 1765	Erastus Willcox Feby 26 1775	
Elijah born	Aug 26th 1767	Sena born May 17 1777	

Peter Willcox Married to Tabitha Davis Feb, 1779 —
Phebe born July 10th 1779   Electa born March 2d 1781

Children of Peter Willcox Jr & Polly his wife

Jerusha	born Sept	10th 1784	Lee
Polly	born Apl	29 1786	Lee
Rhoda	born October 16th 1788		Warrens bush
Oziel	born Jany	9th 1791	Warrens-bush
Peter	born July	2d 1793	Warrens bush —

Children of Ephriam Williams & Mima his Wife

Nancy C— born Feb 16, 1800   Thomas G.   born March 16, 1811
Lucretia W. " Feb. 8, 1805   Thankful C. — March 14, 1815

Children of Josiah Willoughby and Sally his wife

Polly born March 29—1794 —— Lydia born July 27—1796

Children of Jacob Winegar and Anne his wife.

Zacheus born May 10th 1798
Anna Clarena Born June 2d 1800
Anne born June 16th 1802.

Children of Jacob Winegar & Sally his 2d wife

Oliver West born Augt 8th 1804.	Elizabeth	—	Feb. 19, 1811.
Sophronia born July 2d 1805.	Jacob	—	July 30. 1813..
Thankful Nov. 15th 1806.	Sally	—	Oct 31, 1815.
Loisa born June 5th 1809.			

Children of John Winegar & Betsey his wife

Caty	born	May	31—1765.			
Sam!		Feb.	11—1767			
Zacheus		Novr	25—1768	Died March 4—179 †		
Jacob		July	18—1773	Jesse	Feb.	11—1780
Huldah		Aug.	31—1774	David	Jany	8—1781
Betsey		Apl	6—1775.	Stephen	Novr	13—1784
John		June	10—1777	Electa	Aug.	10—1786

Children of Sam! Winegar & Tabitha his wife

John born Septr 19th 1797. Elizabeth March 3d 1799

Samuel Wood and Azubah his Wife

Christian Wood son to Samuel Wood and Azubah his wife Born february the 24th AD: 1775 ——

Azubah Wood Daughter to Samuel Wood and Azubah his Wife born March 30th 1777

Children of Jeremiah Wormer and Keshe his wife

Polly	born	Novr	20—1773.	Richard	Decr	12—1784
Mime		March	1—1776	Laurance February 11—1790		
Hannah		Aug—	10—1779			

Children of Joseph & Elizabeth Wyllys

Huldah born Feb. 17th 1787

Rhoda — Feb. 11th 1790 and Died Apl 10th 1790

Elizabeth Apl 10th 1792. And Died May 8th 1792

Maria — May 26th 1793

William Augustus born Octr 8th 1795

Children of Capt Josiah Yale & Ruth his Wife.

Eunice Yale born July	7th 1777	John	born	July 13—1788
Betsey — — May	28th 1779	Lucy Tracy —		Octr 24—1791
Ruth — — Jany	18th 1782	Electa	—	Aug. 22—1794
Cyrus Yale born May	17th 1786	Josiah	—	July 29—1796

† Last figure obliterated, but the date on the stone over his grave is 1791.

Deaths.

The necrology of the early years of the town is very brief. The inscriptions on a few crumbling stones in the cemeteries, and the short list of deaths given in connection with the family birth records, contain it all until 1792, when Dr. Hyde commenced his admirable Church Records, included in which is a carefully recorded list of deaths which occurred in town during his pastorate.

The death of Pelatiah West is given after the birth record of Elijah and Marah West's children, and the deaths of several of the Crocker family, after the birth record of Joseph and Polly Crocker's children; but except as connected with the records of births, there is no registry of a death on the Town Records until that of Molly Casey, May, 1795, and there is no other recorded until 1797. Scattered here and there on several of the pages allotted to the birth records, are entries of some of the deaths in town between 1797 and 1804—the list of 1799 being nearly complete. In 1804 a systematic record was commenced, and has been continuously kept. These scattered entries, and also those deaths noticed in the preceding Records of Births, are here arranged chronologically. The latter are designated by the page on which they are printed being placed after them; the others are printed as recorded. Some of the dates and ages given in this record, Dr. Hyde's, and in the inscriptions in the cemeteries do not correspond. These are noted if the discrepancy is considerable.

1775.
Sept. 18—Nathaniel, s. of Stephen and Lydia Tobey, æ. 8 d. P. 38.

1777.
Oct. 8—Lydia, d. of Jonathan and Elizabeth West, æ. 1 yr. P. 39
Oct. 17 David, s. of Jonathan and Elizabeth West, æ. 2 y., 4 m. P. 39.

1778.
May 30 Jerusha, w. of Peter Wilcox, æ 39 y., 6 m. P. 41.
May— Esther, d. of Aaron and Marah Benedict, P. 15.

1779.
Jan. 19—Child of Jonathan and Elizabeth West, æ. 2 d. P. 39.
May 16- Jedediah, s. of Nathan and Lucy Davis, æ. 14 d. P. 20.
July 13—Eunice, d. of Aaron and Marah Benedict, æ. 2 d. P. 15.

1780.
June 28— Thomas, s. of Elisha and Elizabeth Freeman, æ. 3 y. P. 24.
Nov. 10—Stephen, s. of John and Lois Nye, æ. 2 m., 19 d. P. 32.
Nov. ——Sarah, d. of Nathan and Lucy Davis, æ. about 7 m. P. 20.
Dec. 9—Jerusha, d. of Jonathan and Deliverence Foot. P. 24.

["Jerusha died Jan 7th 1781, aged 7 Months".—See p. 87.]

1781.

July——Child of Jonathan and Elizabeth West. P. 29.

Dec. 1 Esther, d. of John and Lois Nye, æ. 1 m. P. 32.

1782.

Feb. 5—Marcy, d. of Levi and Temperence Chase, æ. 4 w. P. 18.

1783

May 10—Daniel, s. of Daniel and Hannah Church, æ. 10 y., 11 m. P. 18.

May ——Seth, s. of Levi and Temperence Chase. P. 18.

Oct. 17—Dorse, d. of Amos and Susan Roberts, æ. 1 y., 7 m P. 35.

1784.

Feb. 16—Daniel, s. of Daniel and Hannah Church, æ. 5 m., 8 d. P. 18.

Feb. 20—Samuel, s. of Samuel and Prudence Porter, æ. 4 y. 7 m. P. 34.

Apl. 15—Hannah, w. of Daniel Church. P. 18.—[—" in the 44th year of her age."—See p. 80.]

Aug. 1—Sarah, d. of Nathan and Ruhamah Ball, æ. 11 y., 3 m. P. 13.
[Date of death, and age taken from inscription in the cemetery.—See p. 76.]

Oct. 4—John, s. of Archalaus and Sarah Chadwick, æ. 1 y., 11 m. P. 17.

1785.

Jan. 22—Elizabeth, d. of Daniel and Elizabeth West, æ. 9 y. P. 39.

Mar. 19—Nancy, d. of Cornelius Jr. and Abigail Bassett, of small pox, æ. 1 y., 19 d. P. 15.

May 15—Jared, s. of Elisha and Marah Grant, æ. 2 y., 8 m. P. 25.

Nov. 19 Eunice, w. of Moses Ingersoll in the 50th yr. of her age. P. 31.
[The inscription in cemetery (see p. 80), and Dr. Hyde's record give 1795 as the year of death, and both state in the 51st year of her age.]

1786.

Abijah, s. of John and Lucy Starnes. P. 36.

["A Bijah Son to Mr john Starn's Died June 27th AD 1789 in y 5 ye ar of his age."—See p 91.]

1787.

Mar. 27 - Oziel, s. of Peter and Jerusha Willcox, Killed at Sheffield, æ. 27 y., 7 m., 11 d. P. 41. [See introductory notes.]

May 22—Ira, s. of John and Lois Nye. P. 32.

Pelatiah West Died July—11—1787——

Aug. 20—Samuel, s. of Archalaus and Sarah Chadwick, æ. 1 y., 5 m., 24 d. P. 17.

1788.

Mar. 16—Huldah, w. of Caleb Walker. P. 38.

May 1—Rebeca, d. of Wait and Marah Hatch, æ. about 32 y. P. 27.

1789.

Mar. 12   Parmelia, d. of Elijah and Marah West, æ. 1 y., 6 m., 13 d. P. 39.
Apl. 18—Child of Abraham and Temperence Perry, æ. 15 d. P. 34.
May 23—Child of Joseph and Eunice Bradley—"Died immediately". P. 16.
July 5—Marcy. d. of Samuel and Hannah Tilley, æ. 1 y., 15 d. P. 38.

1790.

Apl. 10—Rhoda, d. of Joseph and Elizabeth Wyllys, æ. 2 m. P. 42
July 11—Marah, w. of Aaron Benedict. P. 15.
               [—"in the 34th year of her age."—See p. 87.] .
July 27—Mary, d. of William and Sarah Whitney, æ. 1 m. P. 40.
July 31--Charity, w. of Col. Jared Bradley. P. 16.
               [—"in the 32d year of her age."—See p. 87.]
Aug. 13—Desire, w. of Abiathar Chadwick, P. 17.
               [—"in the 35th year of her age". See p. 78.]
          Caleb Walker Died at Genessee in the Summer of 1790.—P. 38.
Sep. 8—Betsey, d. of George and Betsey Bennet, æ. 5 m. P. 15.
Dec. 14—Lydia, d. of Jonathan and Elizabeth West, æ. about 2 y. P. 39.
Dec. 22—John, s. of Jonathan and Anne Graves, æ. 1 d. P. 26.

1791.

Jan. 27—Child of Jesse Jr. and Lucy Bradley. P. 16.
Mar. 4—Zacheus, s. of John and Betsey Winegar. P. 42.
               [—"in the 23d year of his age".—See p. 89.]
Apl.   —Patty, d. of Levi and Bathsheba West, æ. about 8 y., 8 m. P. 40.
July   Child of Cornelius and Remember Bassett. P. 14.
July 27—Tabitha, d. of Levi and Temperence Chase, æ. 20 d. P. 18.
Oct. 25—John, s. of Jonathan and Deliverence Foot, æ. 5 m. P. 24.
               [Date given in inscription in cemetery is Oct. 9, 1791:—see p. 87.]
Nov. 1—Polly, d. of Jonathan and Sarah Finney, æ. 2 y., 12 d. P. 23.

1792.

Jan. 5—Erastus, s. of John and Jehannah Gifford, æ. 1 w. P. 25.
May 8—Elizabeth, d. of Joseph and Elizabeth Wyllys, æ. 4 w. P. 42.
          Hannah Crocker Died June 18—1792 in the 60th year of her age.
Oct. 13   David, s. of David and Betsey Foot, æ. 8 m. P. 23.
Nov. 2—Thomas, s. of Levi and Sarah Nye. P. 33.
               [—"in the 19th year of his age".—Date of death and age taken from
               inscription in cemetery :—see p. 81.]
Dec. 17—Child of James and Lucretia Stevens—died day of birth. P. 36.

1793.

Mar. 16   Child of Reuben and Nabby Barlow. P. 14.
Apl. 21   Child of John and Salome Crosby, æ. 4 w. P. 20.
June 28   Sally, d. of John and Sarah Hulett, æ. 4 m., 1 w. P. 29.
Aug. 26   Zafue, s. of James and Achsah Austin, æ. 18 m. P. 12.
Oct.   ——William, s. of Jonathan Jr. and Deliverence Foot, P. 24.
               ["William died Oct 1st 1792 aged 5 weeks". See p. 87.]
Nov. 13   Deliverence, w. of Ichabud Backus, P. 12.
Dec. 4—Isaac, s. of Laurence and Christeen Vandusen, æ. 9 m. P. 38.

1794.

Feb. 8—Wealthy, d. of John and Sarah Hulett. P. 29.
Mar. 13—Huldah, d. of Levi G. Porter, æ. 8 y., 13 d. P. 34.
Mar. 19—Eunice, d. of Elisha and Marah Grant, æ. 2 y., 11 m., 2 d. P. 25.
June 29—Jesse, s. of John and Jehannah Gifford, æ. 1 y., 4 m., 10 d. P. 25.
Peter Willcox Jr born at Richmond July 12th 1765 and died in Grenville of 48 hours illness of the billious Cholic July 16th AD 1794 in the thirtieth year of his age.

1795.

Feb. 15—Polly, d. of Silas and Rachel Easton, æ. 16 d. P. 22.
Mar. 28—Marcy, w. of Paul Ewer. P. 22.
[Date and age from inscription in cemetery:—"March 16th 1795 in the 39th year of her age".—See p. 79.]
Widow Abigail Crocker died Apl 10—1795 in the 90 Year of her age.
Apl. 11—Lewis, s. of John and Jehannah Gifford, æ. 4 d. P. 25.
Apl. 17—Barnabas, s. of Nathaniel and Deborah Tobey, æ. 1 m. P. 23.
May 1—Child of John and Salome Crosby, æ. 11 d. P. 20.
Molly Casey Died May 1795.—["May 5th aged 24 y." Dr.Hyde's record.]
June 5—Rhoda, d. of Levi G. Porter—in her 4th year. P. 34.
Aug. 20—Rebeca, d. of Jonathan and Anne Graves, æ. 2. y. P. 26.
Sep. 7—Marcy Hamlin, d. of Joseph Jr. and Polly Crocker—in her 4th year. P. 19.
Jonathan West Died Septr 1795. P. 39.
Nov. 10—Polly, d. of Elisha and Marah Grant, æ. 2 y., 17 d. P. 25.

1796.

Joseph Crocker Jr died Jany 8—1796 in the 30th Year of his age. P. 19.
Feb. 20—Elizabeth, w. of John Keep. P. 31.
[—"in the 40th year of her age."—Dr. Hyde's record.]
Mar. 6—Charles, s. of John and Lois Nye, æ. 2 m. P. 32.
Mar. 7—Kimbal, s. of Samuel and Prudence Porter. P. 34.
[The inscription in cemetery (see p. 91), and Dr. Hyde give 15 months as the age, which does not correspond with the record on page 34. Probably he was born in 1794 instead of 1795, as there given.]
Apl. 23—Richard, s. of William and Sarah Whitney, æ. 1 y., 2 m., 13 d. P. 40.
Capt. Thomas Crocker died July 5—1796 in the 62 Year of his age —
July 24—Joseph, s. of Joseph and Polly Crocker, æ. 7 m., 20 d. P. 19.
Sep. 17—Child of Reuben and Nabby Barlow—died day of birth. P. 14.
Oct. 15—John, s. of John and Sarah Hulett, æ. 8 y., 1 m., 20 d. P. 29.

1797.

Jan. 2—Betsey, d. of Seth and Bethiah Burden, æ. 5 y., 1 m. P. 17.
Jan. 17—Child of Abraham and Huldah Finney—died day of birth. P. 22.
Jan. 21—Sarah, w. of John Hulet. P. 161. [—"aged 33 yrs."—Dr. Hyde's rec.]
       Pegg Casey died Feb. 16—1797—["-in the 16th year of her age."—Dr. Hyde's record.]
       Ebenezer Chadwick Jr Died Feb,y 25th 1797—
                        [—"in the 25th year of his age."—Dr. Hyde's record.]
Mar. 7—Betsey, d. of William and Jerusha Freeman, æ. 12 d. P. 24.
Apl. 6—Thomas, s. of Josiah and Hannah Crocker, æ. 3. w. P. 20.
May 26—Child of Ancel and Hannah Bassett, æ. 20 d. P. 14.
       Eleazer Turner Died at Lee July 29th 1797.—
                        [—"in the 30th year of his age."—Dr. Hyde's record.]
       Died at Lee Aug. 30 Widow Silence Chase.
                        [—"in the 76th year of her age."—Dr. Hyde's record.]
Sep. 22—Child of Eleazer Turner Died Septr 22d 1797 aged 6 months.
Oct. 23—William Finney, s. of Cornelius and Mercy Hamlin, æ. 1 y., 4
       m. P. 26.
       Mr David Perrys wife died Decr 19th 1797 [See pp. 74, 85.]
       Mr Nathan Ball Died Decr 29th 1797 in the 61st Year of his age.

1798.

Jan. 19—Harriet, d. of Cornelius and Abigail Bassett, æ. 2 y., 9 d. P. 15.
       Mr John Winegar died March 14th 1798—
                        [—"Aged 55 years & 2 M"—See p. 89.]
       Mr Benjamin Hamlin Died May 2d 1798—
                        [—"in the 67th year of his age."—See p. 91.]
May 4—Child of James and Achsah Austin—died day of birth. P. 12.
       Dennis Casey Died may 6th 1798 —
                        ["aged 20 years."—Dr. Hyde's record.]
       Anner Bassett Daughter of Nathan Bassett Died June 5th 1798
                        [—"aged 18 years."—See p. 77.]
       Katharine Winegar Died June 13th 1798 —
                        [—"aged 33 years & 13 days".—See p. 89.]
       Cynthia Chadwick Died July 28th 1798 -
                        [—"aged 13 years."—Dr..Hyde's record.]
       Zeruiah Crocker Died Septr 2d 1798 —
                        [—"in the 21st year of her age".—See p. 78.]
Dec. 23—Betsey Crosby, d. of Josiah and Hannah Crocker, æ. 8 m., 20 d.
       P. 20.

1799.

Jan. 3—Roxe, d. of Abraham and Esther Howk—in her 4th yr. P. 28.
       Phineas Graves's wife Died Jany 7th 1799
       Remember Tobey Died Feb. 7th 1799—
                        [—"in the 22 year of her age."—See p. 75.]
       Widow Elizabeth Turner Died Feb. 20th 1799 —
                        ["aged 30 years."—Dr. Hyde's record.]

Congregational Church Records.

[Many matters are omitted from the Records here printed, but all the Admissions to the Church, the Baptisms, and Dr. Hyde's list of Marriages and Deaths are given.]

Lee May, 25 AD. 1780:

The Professors of religion in the town of Lee met and formed themselves into a Church, The Revd Mr Daniel Collins of Lansborough being present at their request to assist in forming them:

The Church being then formed made choice of Mr Wilm Ingersoll for their Moderator: after which they made choice of Mr Wilm Ingersoll, Mr Jesse Bradley and Mr Prince West as a Committee to sign Letters missive to the Churches in Sheffield, Egremont, Stockbridge, Lenox, Pittsfield, Lansborough, and Williamstown to request their assistance by Pastors and Delegates in the Ordination of Mr Abraham Fowler to the work of the Ministry and pastoral charge of the Church to be on June 8, AD. 1780. On the 6 day of July, Sarah the wife of Levi Nye, Phebe the Wife of Thomas Beecher, Tabitha the wife of Peter Willcocks, Eunice the Wife of Moses Ingersoll, Lydia the wife of Aaron Ingersoll and David Ingersoll were all received as members of full Communion with this Church: The same day Truman son to James Penoyer was baptized.

December 3. Hopestill son to Thomas Beecher was baptized.

December 17. James Penoyer, Daniel Church, and Hannah his wife were received into full Communion with this Church.

December 31. Lois the Wife of Joseph Handy and Elizebeth the Wife of Seth Barlow were received into full Communion with this Church.

Jan. 17. AD. 1781. Heman and Amey Children to Prince West, and Elenor, Anna, Luther, and John-Calvin Children to Moses Ingersoll were baptized.

Jan. 28. Levi Nye, and Hannah the Wife of Hope Davis were received into full Communion with this Church.

Febry 25. John Crosby, and Martha his Wife, Elizebeth Chadwick, and Thankfull the Wife of John Goodspeed were received into full Communion with this Church.

April 22. AD. 1781. Electa Daughter to Peter Willcocks and Benjamin son to James Young were baptized.

June 23. AD. 1782. Abigail Wife to Elisha Goodspeed was received into full Communion with this Church, and she and hir Daughter thankfull were baptized.

August the 4. Josiah Bartholomew, Desire Wife of Abiathar Chadwick, and Moriah Backus were received into full Communion with this Church: Moriah Backus, Billy and Betey Children to Moses Ingersoll, and Daniel Son to Nathan Ball were baptized the same day.

These are the accounts recorded of the Church by Mr Wilᵐ Ingersoll while Moderator of the Church.

July 3, AD. 1783. Mr Elisha Parmele was ordained to the work of the Gospel ministry and pastoral charge of this Church.

The members of this church and their children that are baptized are these that follow.

Josiah Bartholomew Phebe his Wife.

Their Children
Oliver Bartholomew
Phebe Bartholomew
Jesse Bartholomew

Hope Davis Hannah Davis

Willᵐ Ingersoll Lydia Ingersoll

their Children
Moses Ingersoll
Aaron Ingersoll
Barsheba Ingersoll
Jared Ingersoll
David Ingersoll
Willᵐ Ingersoll
Lucinda Ingersoll
Elijah Ingersoll
Calvin Ingersoll
Betcy Ingersoll

Jesse Bradley Mary Bradley.

Their Children.
Jared Bradley
Eli Bradley
Jesse Bradley
Mamry Bradley
Joseph Bradley
William Bradley
Lemi Bradley
Lydia Bradley
Daniel Bradley

Oliver West Thankful West

Their Children
Amy West
Caleb West
Amasa West
Anna West
Sarah West
Joshua West
Oliver West

† S. e 1 . lus.

Lemuel Hatch Temperance Hatch

Their Children
Oliver Hatch
Timothy Hatch
Joseph Hatch
Lemuel Hatch
Ebenezer Hatch
Tempe Hatch
Jonathan Hatch

Prince West

his Children
Barsheba-West
Hannah-West
John West
Silvanus West
Christopher West
Heman West
Amey West
Philo West

Joseph Totman

his Children
Sarah Totman
Elizebeth Totman
Mary Totman
Benjamin Totman

Nathan Ball S Ruhannah Ball

Their Children
Nathan Ball
Lydia Ball
Mary Ball
Sarah Bell
Elizebeth Ball
Martha Ball
John Ball
Anna Ball
James Ball
Samuel Ball
Cesar.

John Crosby   Martha Crosby

Their Children
John Crosby
Abijah Crosby
Hannah Crosby
Thomas Crosby
Abner Crosby
Elizebeth Crosby

Lemuel Crocker   Sarah Crocker

their Children
Samuel Crocker

Levi Nye   Sarah Nye

their Children
Joshua Nye
Benjamin Nye
Mary Nye
Rachel Nye
Thomas Nye
Levi Nye
Sarah Nye

James Penoyer   Sarah Penoyer

their Children
David-lovel Penoyer
Reuben Penoyer
Jacob Penoyer
truman Penoyer
Zina Penoyer

Daniel Church   Hannah Church

Their Children
Rachel Church
Levi Church
Eli Church
Daniel Church

Phinehas Fish   Marcy Fish

Their Children
Joseph Fish — born Decr 20, 1767.
Job Fish — born Decr 2, 1769.
Phinehas Fish— born July 9, 1771.
Samuel Fish — born Sepr 9, 1773.
Elizebeth Fish – born Novr 1, 1776.
Bethia Fish — born Aprl 5, 1779.
Susannah Fish– born Febr 17, 1781.
Thankful Fish– born Febr 11, 1783.

David Kellogg   Elenor Kellogg

their Children
baptized ⎫ Lydia Kellogg
in the   ⎬ Rhoda Kellogg
half way ⎭ Russell Kellogg
       Adosha Kellogg
       David Kellogg
Welthy Kellogg
Hannah Kellogg
Ira Kellogg
Otis Kellogg

David Ingersoll   Sarah Ingersoll

Children
Erastus Ingersoll

James Youngs   Hannah youngs

their Children
James Youngs
Rebekah Youngs
Hannah Youngs
Lydia Youngs
Elizebeth Youngs
Benjamin Youngs
David Youngs
Anna Youngs

Thomas Ewer   Mary Ewer

their Children
Thomas Ewer
Ebenezer Ewer
Ansel Ewer
Lydia Ewer
Seth Ewer
Elisha Ewer

Sarah Foot   Wife of Jonathan Foot

Caty Perry   Wife of Arthur Perry.

her Children
Ruth Perry
Cloe Perry
Mary Perry
Johannah Perry
Abraham Perry
Abigail Perry

Elizebeth Winegar   Wife of John Winegar. her Children
   Catharinah Winegar
   Samuel Winegar
   Zachariah Winegar
   Jacob Winegar
   Huldah Winegar
   Elizebeth Winegar
   John Winegar
   Jesse Winegar
   David Winegar
   Stephen Winegar

Elizebeth Chadwick
   her Children
   Rose Chadwick
   Abiathar Chadwick
   Archelus Chadwick
   Samuel Chadwick

Hannah Collins Wife of Oliver Collins.
   her Children
   Elisha Collins
   Archebal Collins
   Oliver Collins
   Avis Collins
   Elias Collins
   John Collins
   Isaac Collins

Tryphena Marsh   Wife of Reuben Marsh. her Children
   Judith Marsh

Tabitha Willcocks   Wife of Peter Willcocks. her Children
   Mary Davis
   Thomas Davis
   Anna Davis
   Rowland Davis
   Epraim Davis
   Timothy Davis
   Phebe Willcocks
   Electe Willcocks

Desire Chadwick Wife of Abiathar Chadwick. her Children
   Fear Chadwick
   Heman Chadwick
   Joseph Chadwick

Thankfull Goodspeed   Wife of John Goodspeed. her Children
   Obed Goodspeed

Eunice Ingersoll   Wife of Moses Ingersoll. her Children
   Elenor Ingersoll
   Anna Ingersoll
   Luther Ingersoll
   John-Calvin Ingersoll
   Billy Ingersoll
   Betcy Ingersoll

Moriah Backus
   her Children
   Hannah Backus
   Sarah Backus
   Nathaniel Backus
   Anson Backus
   Benjamin Backus

Sarah Chadwick   Wife of Archelus Chadwick. her Children
   Thomas Chadwick
   Jabez Chadwick
   Elizebeth Chadwick
   John Chadwick

Lydia Ingersoll   Wife of Aaron Ingersoll. her Children
   Jonathan Ingersoll
   Stephen Ingersoll

Deliverance Foot   Wife of Jonathan Foot. her Children
   Elisha Foot
   Alvin Foot
   Jerusha Foot

Thankfull Dimmuck   Wife of Sylvanus Dimmuck. her Children
   Hannah Dimmuck

Lydia Gifford   Wife of Thomas Gifford   her Children
   Abigail Gifford
   Isaac Gifford
   Huldah Gifford
   Sarah Gifford
   Cornelius Gifford

Catherina Winegar

Naomi Goodspeed   Wife of David
Goodspeed   her Children
   Naomi Goodspeed
   Antony Goodspeed

Mary Hatch   Wife of Wate Hatch
   her Children
   Rebekkah Hatch
   Lewes Hatch
   Priscilla Hatch
   Edward Hatch

Elizebeth West the Wife of Daniel
West.   her Children
   Elizebeth West
   Saviah West
   Thomas-Tracy West
   Daniel West
   Lucy West.

Experience Coffey   Wife of John
Coffey   her children
   Mary Coffey
   Betcy Coffey
   Rachel Coffey
   Crecia Coffey

Phebe the Wife of Thomas Beecher
   her Children
   Hopestill Beecher
   Submit Beecher

Seth & Amy Nye
   their Children
   Elisha Nye

Lois Handy Wife of Joseph Handy
   their Children
   Joseph Handy
   Nathaniel Handy
   Seth Handy

Aaron Benedic
   Children
   Clarissa Benedic
   Stephen-Thomas Benedic

Mary the Wife of Elisha Grant
   Their Children
   Elisha Grant
   Ruth Grant
   Prudence Grant
   Jared Grant

Elizebeth Wife [of] Seth Barlow
   her Children
   Samuel Barlow
   Nathan Barlow

Lydia the Wife of Stephen Toby

Jerusha Standly

Olliver Hatch & Rebekah Hatch
   Their Children.

Thomas Crocker Mercy Crocker.

[Several pages in the original, are blank after the above list, on which evidently, it
was designed that the names of persons taken into the church from time to time,
and their children, should be entered. The list, however, remains as left by Wm.
Ingersoll; the clerks following him, making no additions to it.]

Lee July 18, 1783. The Church agreed to choose two Deacons: and choose M̈r David ingersoll Choirester. [See p. 108.]

July 13. Thankful Fish daughter of Phinehas and Marcy Fish was baptized.

July 20, Hannah Backus, Sarah Backus, Nathaniel Backus, Anson Backus, Benjamin Backus, Children of Moriah Backus: John Chadwick Son of Archelus and Sarah Chadwick: and Fear Chadwick, Heman Chadwick, and Joseph Chadwick, Children of Abiathar and Desire Chadwick were all baptized.

July 24, Mary the Wife of Thomas Yure, and Amy the Wife of Seth Nye were examined by this Church: and propounded with a view to join this Church in full communion on the 26, of July.

July 27. Crecia daughter of John and Experience Coffey was baptized.

August 3, Otis the son of David and Elenor Collogg, Samuel the son of Lemuel and Sarah Crocker, and Elizebeth, Saviah, Thomas-Tracy, Daniel, and Lucy the Children of Daniel and Elizebeth West, were all baptised.

August 10. Mary the Wife of Thomas Ewer and Amey the Wife of Seth Nye were both received into full communion with this Church: and M̈rs Ewer was baptized the same time being not certain that she was baptized in her infancy.

August 29, The Church met and passed the following votes:

1. That no complaint shall be brought before the Church of any member except by the desire of one or two members exclusive of the offended Brother.

2. That no member of another Church shall be allowed to pertake of the Lords supper occationally more than nine months from the time of his becoming an Inhabitant of the Town unless circumstances shall be such as the Church shall judge it proper to vary from this term of time, making the time of Ordination that from which they begin to reckon.

3. That at all Church meetings any Brother being absent or not being there by the time appointed shall be deemed censurable unless he has such reasons as shall by the Church be judged sufficient for his excuse.

August 31. Elisha son of Seth and Amy Nye was baptised.

September 4. The Church chos M̈r Oliver West and M̈r Jesse Bradley to the Office of Deaconship.

Sepẗr 7. Samuel son of Nathan and S. Ruhamah Ball was baptised.

Sepẗr 21. Lydia Wife of William Ingersoll, Phebe the Wife of Josiah Bartholomew, Aaron Benedic, Mary Wife of Elisha Grant, Lydia Wife of Stephen Toby, and Jerusha Standly were received into full communion with this Church: and M̈rs Toby with Thomas, Ebenezer, Ansel, Lydia, Seth and Elisha Children of Thomas and Mary Ewer, were all baptized.

September 28. Nathan son of Seth and Elizabeth Barlow was baprized.

October 5. Clarissa and Stephen-Thomas children of Aaron Benedic were baptized.

October 12. Elisha, Ruth, Prudence, Jared Children of Elisha and Mary

Grant were baptized.

November 2. Olliver Hatch and Rebekah his Wife were received into full Communion with this Church.

November 23. Thomas Crocker and Marcy his Wife and also Sarah the Wife of David Ingersoll were received into full communion with this Church.

———

January 15, AD. 1784. Daniel son of Daniel and Hannah Church was baptized, being sick and not likely to live he was baptized at his Fathers house.

Jan. 18. Stephen son of John and Elizebethe Winegar was baptized.

February 6. The Church met and passed the following Votes:

1. That when any matter is to be decided by the Church, no Person exclusive of the Church shall be present while they are deciding the matter.

2. That it is their opinion, that there is an absolute and certain connexion between the faithfulness of believing Parents in training up their children and the Salvation of the Children thus trained up:

That this their opinion arises from their supposing that this connexion is graciously made in the Covenant of Grace.

[The preceding Rec r 's were wri ten by Wm. Ingersoll, whose hand does not appear again. The next entries are supposed to be in Deacon Jesse Bradley's writing]

May 13. The Church met and passed the following Vote: viz Takeing into consideration the circumstances of Mr Parmele as to his low and declining state of health — —

Voted that we are willing he should take a journey to Virginia with a view to recover health.

May ye 18. At a church meeting; after consulting with Mr Parmele and takeing into view his state of health and his desire to journey into the southern states—We do mutually agree and vote that he shall be at liberty to settle amongst any people (should he ever recover such a measure of health as to be able): likewise we on our part are at liberty to call and settle a nother Minister.

[Here the Records commence in a different hand, supposed to be Deacon Oliver West's. Except when otherwise noted, the remainder of the 1st book is in this hand. The first entry below is not the next in order in the original, but is next in time.

Lee August ye 8th 1781 Mr Monson Preachd and Adminnestred the Sacrament here Seth Nye was Receved into ful communion with this Church and was baptized Ezekiel Son of Prince and Hannah West Salle daughter of Daniel and Elizabeth west and Esther and David Children of Elisha and Mary Grant and Remembrance Celah and Stephen Children of Stephen and Lidia Toby ware all baptized

December ye 5th Mr Monson Adminnestred the Sacrament and Baptized   † of Thomas and Phebe Beacher and Mary daughter of Abiather [and] Desire Chadwick and John Son of Achelus and Sarah Chadwick ——

† Probably the space should have been filled by: "Submit, daughter." See p. 53.

January the 9th 1785 Mr West Adminnestred the Sacrament Jesse Gifford and Ruth his Wife Samuel Davis and Priscilla his Wife Josiah Yale and Ruth his Wife Sarah the Wife of Roswel Hubbort Cornelus Bassett and Archelus Chadwick all were recvd into the Church and Jesse Gifford and Samuel Davis †Mary and Hopestill Children of Samuel and Priscilla Davis all were baptized.

August the 14th 1785 Mr Kirkland Preached here and baptized Isaac Son of Nathan and Ruhamah Ball and Lucina daughter of Aaron Benedic and Eli Son of Oliver Hatch and Elisha and John Sons of Cornelius Bassett

Lee June ye 25th 1786 Mr Monson preachd here and Baptized Theodor Son of David and Sarah Ingersol and Elisha Parmale Son of Samuel and Prissilla Davis

September the 17th 1786 Mr Perry Preached here and administred the Sacrament and Baptized Electa daughter of John and Elizebath Winegar and Lidia daughter of Stephen and Lidia Toby, and Ira Son of Daniel and Elizabeth West Thankful daughter of Elisha and Mary Grant and Sirus Son of Josiah and Ruth Yale Archelus Son of Abiather and Desire Chadwick Daniel Lewes Son of oliver and Rebekah Hatch and Samuel Son of Archelus and Sarah chadwick, and Elizabeth Wife of Cornelius Gifford and Eunice Wife of Ebenezar Brown were taken into the church

Sabathday june the 10th 1787 Mr Camp Preachd here and Baptized Prince Son of Prince and Hannah West and David Son of Cornelus Basset and Lucy daughter of John and Lucy Williams was given up by Jerusha Standly and ‡ Thomas and Mary Ewer‡

April 6th 1788 Mr Averry preachd here and Baptized Lucreace daughter of David and Sarah Ingersol

April the 20th Mr Bell baptized Caleb Son of Seth and Amy Nye

May the 4th Mr Steevens Baptized Hannah daughter of Dannel and Ann Church and Jonathan Son of Jonathan and Deliverance Foot

Sabathday June ye 1—1788 Mr West preached att Lee and baptized Elisebeth daughter of Daniel and Elizebeth West.

Sabathday August the 24 Mr West Preached here and baptized Nathaniel Son of Stephen [and] Lydia Toby

February the 22 1789 Mr Sanford preached here and baptized Ezra Son of James and Hannah Youngs and Sarah Daughter of Archelus and Sarah Chadwick

Lee March the 16th 1789 the church met and voted unanimusly to desire Mr William Fowler Miller to take the Pastoral Care and Charg of this Church Provided the Town will unite in Supporting him

† The name "Sally," instead of Mary, is given on p. 20.

‡ See p. 51. Seth and Elisha Ewer were baptized Sept. 21, 1783. Probably the name of a later child should have been here inserted, and obviously, "was baptized," was also omitted.

June the 20th 1790 Mr Monson Preached hear and administred the Sacrament and John Son of Josiah Yale and Moses Son [of] David and Sarah Ingersol and Thankfull Daughter of Seth and Amy Nye all were baptized

July the 29 the Church met and voted to Desire Hope Davis Nathan Ball & Prince West to go and Converse With Mrs Bradley and inquire the Reason of her not attending our meeting and also to Converse with Mr Penoy[e]r respecting his Ideas of all mankinds being finaly happy

August the 1 Mr Avery Preachd here and Eleaser Son of Thomas Ewer Aaron & Desire children of Aaron Bennedick and Lemuel & David children of Oliver Hatch all were baptized

october the first day Mr Avery preached a lecter here and baptized +of Samuel and Prissilla Davis

September the 18th 1791 Mr Shaw Preached here and Baptized Pamela daughter of Thomas and Phebe Beacher Orson Son of Daniel and Elisebeth West and Eunes Daughter [of] Elisha [and] Mary Grant and John son of Joua[t]han [and] Deliverence Foot and September 25 he baptized anna daughter of Daniel and anna Church and Elizabeth daughter of Thomas and Mary Ewer and Alvin Son of James and Hannah youngs

Novr 20th Mr Monson Preached in this town, & baptized Charlotte, daughter of Lucy Bullard.

[This last item above, is in the Rev. Alvan Hyde's writing.]

February 23d 1792 the Church met and voted unanimusly to give Mr Alvin Hide a call to take the Pasteral Care and Charge of the Church

Sabathday may 6 Mr Avery preached here & adminnestered the Sacrament and baptized Abraham Phebe Thomas Lidia & Abigail Children of jesse and Ruth Gifford and Asel Son of Stephen and Lydia Toby and Soffe Daughter of David and Sarah Ingersol and betsy Daughter of Seth & Amy Nye and Ruth Daughter of Archelus and Elizebeth Chadwick

---

† See p. 20. The three oldest children having been baptized (Jan. 29, 1785) and June 25, 786.) perhaps Rebecca and Samuel were baptized at this time.

[Ordination of Mr. Elisha Parmele.]

At an ecclesiastical Counsel conveined at Lee pursuant to Letters missmive received from the Church of Christ in said Town, requesting our assistance in setting apart Mr Elisha Parmele to the pastoral Office over them in the Day 3rd of June AD 1783. Present

Elders Rev. Messrs ——	Delegates
Stephen West, Stockbridge	Elijah Brown Esq
Daniel Collins, Lanesborough	Samuel Durham
Thomas Allen, Pittsfield	Josiah Bright — —
Samuel Munson, Lenox.	John Stoughton
Eliphalet Steel, Egremont	Eberer Olds —— — —
Zadock Hurn,‡ Becket	Isaiah Kingsley
Joseph Avery, Alford.	Robert Johnson — —
Seth Swift Wut†	Benjamin Skinner

Docke West was chosen Moderator and Mr. Collins Scribe, the Counsel was opened by prayer seeking to God for Counsel and direction in the important Matters to be laid before them. ——

The Counsel then gave a full and candid hearing to a paper laid before them signed by 21 of the inhabitants of the town, containing a request that the Counsel would not proceed to ordain Mr Parmele to the work of the Gospel Ministry in this place, [in] which also their reasons against it were stated. — After which the Counsel proceeded to a strick and carefull Examination of the Candidate, and were unanimously agreed that he appeared to be a person duely qualified for the important Office of the Gosp Ministry and after carefully deliberating the Objections which were made against Mr Parmeles being set apart to the pastoral Office amongst them the Council were of the Opinion that these Objections sentered in a Disapprobation of Mr Parmeles religious Sentiments, and that his Sentiments were in their Judgement strictly founded on scripture so that they judjed these objections to be groundless: the Counsel wer of opinion they ought to proceed to the Ordination of Mr Parmele and did accordingly set him apart by prayer and the true position of hands to the pastoral Office over the Church and people in this Town.

Signed

Stephen West Modr

Test Daniel Collins Scribe

Alvan Hyde Jun 2 Scribe

† Hunn.

‡ Williamstown.

[It may reasonably be supposed that the above account of the ordination of Mr. Parmele was copied into the Recor ls about 25 years after the event, for Alvan Hyde, Jr. was born in 1794, and the writing has the characteristics of that of a boy in his early teens.

The following Church Records are entirely by Dr. Hyde, and contained in a separate book from the preceding.]

THE RECORDS OF THE CHURCH OF CHRIST IN LEE.—

Result of the Council appointed for the ordination of Mr Alvan HyDE.

At an ecclesiastical Council at Lee on the 5th day of June, A. D. 1792 — in consequence of letters missive from the Church in that place[†]in order to set apart Mr Alvan Hyde to the work of the gospel-ministry, & to commit to him the pastoral care of the church, & the administration of the gospel among that people.

Present

Elders.	Delegates from the Churches.
Rev. Stephen West of Stockbridge.	Erastus Sergeant Esqr —
Daniel Collins — Lanesborough.	Mr Eldad King.
Thomas Allen of Pittsfield.	Deacon John Partridge.
Ephraim Judson of Sheffield.	Deacon Aaron Foot.
Eliphalet Steele of Egremont.	Mr Bartholomew Heath.
Charles Backus of Somers.	Mr Charles Sheldon.
David Perry of Richmond.	Deacon James Gates.
Joseph Avery of Tyringham.	Deacon William Hale.
Samuel Nott of Franklin.	Deacon Joshua Willis.
Jacob Catlin New Marlborough.	Col. Daniel Taylor.

The council made choice of Mr West Moderator, & Mr Catlin Scribe — after which the council was opened by prayer by the Moderator.

It was then proposed to attend to the examination of Mr Hyde; & after a most careful examination of his knowledge in the doctrines of the holy scriptures, & of his experimental acquaintance with the religion of Jesus Christ; as also, of his other qualifications for the work of the gospel-ministry, the council voted unanimously that they approve of his qualifications, & proceed to the public solemnities of ordination.

The parts in the public solemnity were assigned to the Reverend Elders in the following manner — viz — Mr Nott to make the introductory prayer, Mr Backus to preach the sermon, Mr Collins to make the consecrating prayer, Mr West to give the charge, Mr Steele to give the right hand of fellowship, and Mr Avery to make the concluding prayer.

June 6th 1792. The council proceeded to a convenient stage erected for the purpose, & in presence of the church & congregation of Lee, & a respectable assembly, solemnly consecrated Mr Hyde to the sacred office of a minister of Christ, & committed to his charge the church of Christ in that place.

Jacob Catlin Scribe ——   Stephen West, Moderator.

† See p. 106.

An account of persons taken into the church of Christ in Lee, since June 6.^h 1792, the time Mr Alvan Hyde was ordained.

June 17th 1792 — Elisha Freeman, & Elizabeth, his wife, Cornelius Bassett & Abigail his wife, Anne the wife of Daniel Church, & Mehitabel, the wife of Andrew West, were all received into this church in full communion.

August 12th 1792 — David Perry, & Desire his wife, Thomas Beecher, Samuel Winegar, Elizabeth West, Temperance Chase the wife of Levi Chase, Abigail Parcival the wife of Elisha Parcival, were all taken into this church in full communion.

Sept 9th 1792. Lewis Hatch, Sarah Dodge the wife of Asel Dodge, & Mercy Ingersol the wife of William Ingersol Junr , were taken into this church.

Oct 14th 1792. — Seth Abbott and Martha his wife, Joseph Bradley and Eunice his wife, Mehitabel Northrop the wife of Thomas Northrop, Elizabeth Crocker the wife of Job Crocker, Nabby Barns, and Miriam Dickinson were received into this Church.

November 11th 1792. — — — Elisha Parcival, Peter Willcox, Nathaniel Hamlin and Abigail his wife, James Austin and Achsah his wife,— Daniel West, Nathaniel Bassett, Daniel Willcox, Asahel Foot, Widow Silence Chase, Phebe Bradley the wife of Eli Bradley, Anne Abbott, and Daniel Santie, and Betsey his wife, were all taken into this Church.

December 9th 1792 — — — Edmund Hinckley and Content his wife, Nathan Davis and Lucy his wife, Paul Ewer and Mercy his wife, Daniel Church, Jared Ingersol, Ebenezer Jenkins Junr , Elizabeth Jenkins the wife of Ebenr Jenkins Esq., Sarah Tuttle ye wife of James Tuttle, & Martha Crocker ye wife of L! Joseph Crocker were all taken into this church.

December 23d 1792. Widow Thankful Dimick was taken into this chh.

January 13th 1793. Jonathan Foot, David Goodspeed, Levi Chase, Solomon Foot, Mehitabel West, the wife of Ebenezer West, Anne Bradley the wife of Heman Bradley, Nabby Barlow the wife of Reuben Barlow, Molly Stanley, Louis Nye, the wife of John Nye, and Joshua and Charity Nye, were all received into the communion and fellowship of this church.

March 10th 1793. Jedidiah Crocker and Sarah his wife, James Tuttle, Samuel Tilley and Hannah his wife Josiah Crocker, Jabez Chadwick, Salvina Baker the wife of David Baker, Deborah Taylor, Sarah-Ann Foot.—Hannah Barlow, and Huldah Winegar, were all received into this Church.

May 5th Nathaniel Toby & Deborah his wife, John Parcival & Ruth his wife, John Nye, Samuel Porter, Ebenezer West, Tabitha Gifford, Zurviah Wells, Ruth Tyler, Joanna Gifford, Thankful Barlow, Olive Thompson, Lucy Hyde, Mary Casey, Lydia Ball, Huldah Gifford & Hannah Dodge, were all received into this church. ——

July 14th Daniel Church, Thomas Fuller Remember Bassett, Sarah Tyler, Tempe Perry, & Lydia Bradley were received into this Church. —

Sept 8th Jeremiah Wormer, Joseph Crocker Senr, Eli Bradley, Elizabeth Bennett, & Eunice Fuller, were all received into this Church. ——

November 17th — John Gifford, Jesse Bradley Junr —William Bradley, Dorcas Crocker, & Zina Penoyer were received to the communion & fellowship of this Church.

1794.

Jany 12th Sarah Lee, the wife of Ashbel Lee, was received into the communion & fellowship of this church. — —

March 21 Enoch Garfield was received to the communion & fellowship of this Church. —— ——

May 18th John Couch Senr & his wife, James Gifford & Sarah his wife,—Mamre Bartholomew, the wife of Jesse Bartholomew, Lydia Hinsdale, & Tabitha Crocker were all received by this church to their fellowship & communion.

July 13th Tabitha Hamblin was received by this church to their communion & fellowship. ——

Decemr 23d Benjamin Backus was received by this church to their communion & fellowship, at his own house, where the church convened, on the account of his being sick. —— ——

1795.

July 12th Ephraim Sheldon, & Mrs Sarah Blackman, wife of Mr Jonth Blackman, were received by this church to their communion & fellowship.

Novr 8th Mr Levi Robinson and ———— his wife were received by this church to their communion & fellowship, being recommended by the church of Christ at Meriden in Connecticut.

1796.

Janny 10th Mrs Prudence Porter, wife of Mr Samuel Porter, was received by this church to their communion & fellowship.

June 7th Mrs Lydia Barlow, wife of Mr Peleg Barlow, was received by this Church to their communion & fellowship, at her own house, where the Church convened on account of her being sick.

Novr 13th Widow Thankful Bassett, and Martha, the wife of Mr Nathl Howland, were received by this Church to their communion and Fellowship, being recommended from the West Church in Barnstable. —

1797.

Samuel Leonard Junr was received by this church to their communion and fellowship, on the 12th day of March — also at the same time widow

Experience Childs was received, by this church, to their communion and fellowship, being recommended from the West Church in Barnstable.——

April 23d Mrs   Hambleton was received, by this church, to their communion and fellowship, being recommended by the Revd Gideon Hawley, Pastor of the church at Marshpee. ———   ——

July 30th Lemuel Barlow and Josiah Willoughby were received, by this church, to their communion & fellowship.

Sept 10th Widow Sarah Parsons, recommended from the church in Stockbridge, and Mrs Prudence Ingersol, recommended from the church in Willington, were recommended to communion —— also Grace Wormer, the wife of Jeremiah Wormer — and Chloe Wansey, the wife of Henry Wansey, were received into the church. ——

1798.

April 22d 1798 Squire Stone and   his wife, recommended from the church at West Stockbridge, were received as members of this church.

Sept 2d Deidama Perry was received by this church to their communion & fellowship.

1799.

Jan-y 13th Abigail Bradley, the wife of Mr Asahel Bradley, was received to the communion and watch of this chh, being recommended from the church at Cornwall, in Connecticut.

March 10th Hannah Crocker, wife Mr Josiah Crocker, was received by this church to their communion, watch and fellowship.

April 14th Abraham Hall, and Rachel, his wife, were received to the communion, watch & fellowship of this Church.

June 30th Esther Bailey,wife of Mr Thomas Bailey,was received to the ommunion and fellowship of this Church.

July 28th Anne Parcival, daughter of Mr Elisha Parcival, was received to the communion and fellowship of this Church.

Sept 8th Dean Rowland Thatcher and his wife were received to the communion and fellowship of this church.

Novr 3d Samuel Couch & Hannah his wife, Stephen Bradley & widow Rebecca Putnam, were received to the communion & fellowship of this church. ——   ——

1800.

Jan-y 12th Prudence Couch, wife of John Couch Junr —Lucy Crocker, wife of Elisha Crocker — Thankful Humphrey, wife of Elias Humphrey and Sally Squire were all received to the communion and fellowship of this Church. ———

March 9th Dr Nathl Thayer & Anne his wife, recommended from the church at Durham, in Connecticut — John Couch Junr — Lydia Bradley, the wife [of] Stephen Bradley — Hannah Davis, the wife of

Calvin Davis — Sarah Stewart, Patience Dexter, Sophia Crocker, Lemira Crocker and Laura Crocker, were all received to the communion and fellowship of this Church.

May 4th John Winegar and Lydia Stanton were received to the communion & fellowship of this Church.

Sept 14th Adria Squire, wife of Ebenr Squire, Rhoda Hatch and Elizabeth Robinson were received to the communion & fellowship of the church.

Octr 19th Samuel Prince Robbins, and Sally Barlow were received to the communion & fellowship of this church. ——

An account of persons baptized by the Revd Alvan Hyde, who was ordained to the work of the Gospel-ministry and charge of this church, June 6th 1792. — —

June 17th Elizabeth Freeman, wife of Elisha Freeman,— Nancy, Lemuel, and Lydia, children of Cornelius Bassett and Abigail his wife, — Hannah and Abigail, children of Mehitabel West, wife of Andrew West— Molly and Betsey, children of Aaron Benedict — and Justus and Oliver, children of Oliver Hatch were all baptized.

June 24th — Elisha, Fanny, Thomas, and Lydia Parcival, children of Elisha Freeman & Elizabeth his wife were baptized.

July 8th Lucy Tracy, daughter of Josiah and Ruth Yale, and Elisha son of Lydia Ingersol, wife of Aaron Ingersol were baptized. [See p. 108.]

July 15th Sarah, Lydia Lemuel and Salvina, children of David Baker were baptized. ——

July 22d —Elizabeth, daughter of Elizabeth Barlow, wife of Seth Barlow, was baptized.

August 5th Priscilla, daughter of Samuel and Priscilla Davis was baptized.

Sept 2d Elisha, Huldah, Fear, Polly & John, children of Elisha & Abigail Parcival were baptized [Deliverance!]

Sept 23d William, son of Jonathan and Melitabel Foot, — Wait, Thomas Davis, Alpheus, and Tabitha, children of Lewis Hatch, — Lydia, Seth Crocker, William, Cela, and Sarah, children of William and Mercy Ingersol — & Darius Carpenter, a child taken to be educated by Thankful Goodspeed— were all baptized. ——— ——

Octob. 14th Elizabeth Crocker, the wife of Job Crocker, Miriam Dickinson, and Heman, Asahel, Sarah and Samuel Stanley, children of Asahel and Sarah Dodge, were baptized. —— ——

Octob. 28th — — Huggins, Betsey, Celah, Electa & Olive, children of Job and Elizabeth Crocker were baptized. ——— —

Novr 4th Asenath, daughter of Joseph & Eunice Bradley was baptized.

Nov! 11th Elisha Parcival, Daniel Willcox, and Asahel Foot were baptized.

Nov! 18th — Deborah-Webb, Hannah, John-Smith, Nabby & Polly, children of Nathaniel & Bethiah Bassett, — Philo, Celah, Anne, Polly & Josiah, children of Eli & Phebe Bradley, — and Berenice & Zafne, children of James & Achsah Austin, were all baptized. ——

Nov! 25th Daniel, son of Miriam Dickinson was baptized. ——

Dec! 9th Content Hinckley the wife of Edmund Hinckley, Lucy Davis the wife of Nathan Davis, Mercy Ewer the wife of Paul Ewer, and Nathaniel, son of Nathaniel and Abigail Hamlin, were all baptized. ——

Dec! 23d Polly, daughter of Lewis Hatch was baptized. — — —

1793.

Jan! 13. Solomon Foot, Nabby Barlow, the wife of Reuben Barlow, Charity Nye, the wife of Joshua Nye, Lucy, Hannah-Crocker, Nathan, Charity-Hall, and Isaac, children of Nathan and Lucy Davis, — — and Ruth, daughter of Jesse and Ruth Gifford were all baptized.

Jan! 27. Hannah, John, Ira, and Esther, children of John and Louis Nye, were baptized.

Feb! 10th Sally, Benjamin, Grissilda, Betsey-Clark, Polly and Asa children of Joseph & Martha Crocker, — and Huldah, James and Polly, children of Daniel Church were baptized. —— —— —

March 3! Stephen, Ephraim, Phebe, Timothy-Nye, & Joel, children of Ebenezer & Mehitabel West were baptized.

March 10th Jedidiah Crocker & Sarah his wife, James Tuttle, Samuel Tilly and Hannah his wife, Salvina Baker the wife of David Baker, Deborah Taylor, and Sarah-Ann Foot, were all baptized.

April 7th Pelatiah, son of Daniel & Elizabeth West, — and Louis daughter of John and Louis Nye were baptized.

May 5th Nathaniel Toby & Deborah his wife, Mary Casey, Hannah Dodge, John Parcival & Ruth his wife, Charles, a son of Elisha & Elizabeth Freeman, & Joel a son of Joseph & Eunice Bradley were all baptized.

June 2d Thomas, son of Cornelius & Abigail Bassett was baptized.

June 9th Sylvanus, Sylva, John, Geneverah & Jesse children of Joanna Gifford, & Rhoda, Hezekiah-Orton, & Chauncey, children of Gideon & Oliver Thompson, were baptized. —— —— ——

June 16th Ebenezer-Nibloo, Polly, Louis, John, David, & Merit, children of Jared Ingersoll were baptized. —— —— ——

June 23d Remember-Nye, a child of Cornelius Bassett, was baptized.

July 14th Lecta & Rhoda, children of Samuel & Hannah Tilly were baptized.

July 21st Sarah, a child of Stephen & Lydia Tobey was baptized. ——

Aug! 4th John-Crocker, Mary-Busley, Tilson, Jane, Nabby and Martha, children of Paul & Mercy Ewer, were baptized. ——

Aug! 11th Elizabeth Handy, a child taken to be educated by Hannah Collins, the wife of Oliver Collins, was baptized. —— ——

Aug! 25th Achsah, Samuel, Mary. Deborah & Cynthia, children of Nathaniel & Deborah Toby —— Noah, Jedediah-Davis, Sarah, Samuel & Elizabeth, children of Jedediah & Sarah Crocker —— Polly, & Arthur, children of Abraham & Tempe Perry were all baptized. —— ——

Sept 8th Asa, son of Thomas, & Mary Ewer — John, Samuel, Ruth, James, Montgomery & Hannah-Gates, children of John & Ruth Parcival — William Bassett, Cornelius, Hannah, & Reuben, children of Thankful Barlow;-Sibyl, David,& Sally, children of Sarah Tyler, were all baptized.

Sept 8. Joseph Crocker was baptized. —— —— ——

Octo. 6th David, son of David & Salvina Baker was baptized. ——

Octobr 20th Betsey Denio, a child taken to be educated by Sarah Dodge, was baptized.

Novr 17th —— John Gifford, —— Mary, Grace, Lorain, Abigail, & Lydia, children of Samuel Porter — Henry-Williams & Pruda, children of Elizabeth Bennett, — & Lucy, Elihu, Jacob, & Thomas-Williams, children of Eunice Fuller, were all bapt ..ed.

Decr 1st Betsey, a child of Jesse Bradley Junr was baptized.   ,

Decr 15th Polly, daughter of Elisha and Mary Grant was baptized.—

1794.

Jany 5th Sally, daughter of Eli & Phebe Bradley was baptized. ——

Jany 12th Ancel, son of Archelaus & Elizabeth Chadwick was baptized.

Feby 23. Tamar, daughter of Oliver Hatch was baptized.

May 4th Reuben, son of Jared Ingersol was baptized. ——

May 18th James Gifford, & Lydia Hinsdale were baptized — also Alvan, son of Jesse & Ruth Gifford, & Sarah-Ann, daughter of Asahel & Anne Foot.

June 1st Alvah, child of Thomas & Phebe Beecher, & Lucy, a child of Samuel & Hannah Tilly, were baptized.

June 15th Daniel, son of Daniel Church Junr, was baptized. ——

July 15th Tabitha Hamblin was baptized. —— ——

July 27th Eunice, daughter of Aaron Benedict, —— Mamre, Jesse-Bradley, Lemi, Augustus & Lydia, children of Mrs Mamre Bartholomew, Nathaniel, son of Nathaniel & Bethiah Bassett, Alvan, son of Alvan & Lucy Hyde, & Henry-William, son of Ebenezer Jenkins Junr & Lydia his wife, were all baptized. ——-

Sept 14th Eunice, daughter of James & Sarah Gifford, was baptized. -

Sept 28th Bathsheba, daughter of Nathan & Lucy Davis,was baptized.

October 19th Electa, daughter of Josiah & Ruth Yale, was baptized. —

Novr 2d Abigail, child of Joseph Crocker Senr was baptized. —— —

Novr 9th Olive, daughter of Gideon & Olive Thompson was baptized.-

Novr 30th Dama daughter of Abraham & Tempe Perry, was baptized.

Decr 14th Amanda, daughter of Jesse Bradley Junr was baptized. ——

Decr 28th Polly, Silas, Daniel, children of Enoch Garfield—& Thomas son of Wm Ingersol Junr & Mercy his wife were baptized. ——

1795.

Jan? 4th Eunice, daughter of Joseph & Eunice Bradley, & Sarah, daughter of Joshua & Charity Nye, were baptized. — — — —

Jan? 11th Kimball Porter, son of Samuel Porter, & Wait-Hatch Davis, son of Samuel & Pris illa Davis, were baptized. — — — —

Jan? 18th Artemesia, a child of Mr Joseph King of Barrington was baptized. — — —

March 19th Was baptized an infant son of Mr Paul Ewer, at his own house, by the name of Paul. — — —

March 25th Nathan, son of Ebenezer Jenkins Jan? was baptized, at his fathers house, being dangerously sick.

April 5th Lucy, a child of Samuel & Lydia.Hodges, was baptized — —

April 12th Content, daughter of John and Ruth Parcival was baptized.

April 19th David and Sarah, twin-children, of Mr David and Sarah Ingersol, were baptized. — — — —

June 14th Lydia, daughter of Ephraim & Lydia Sheldon was baptized.

July 12th Polly, daughter of Jedediah & Sarah Crocker was baptized.-

July 26 th Alvah, son of Daniel & Eliz ibeth West was baptized — —

Aug! 2d Was baptized Elizabeth, daughter of Jared Ingersol. — — —

Octob. 4th Was baptized Cornelius, son of Samuel Barlow.

Oct br 25th Was baptized Joshua, son of Seth & Amy Nye. — — —

Nov? 8th Was baptized Ezra-Thompson, son of Huldah Finney.

Nov? 29th Was baptized Zafne, son of James and Achsah Austin.

Dec? 13th Was baptized Hudson, son of Daniel & Lydia Wilcox.

1796.

Feb? 7th Was baptized Charles, son of John & Louis Nye.

Feb? 14th Was baptized Harriot, daughter of Cornelius & Abigail Bassett, and Elizabeth, daughter of Asael & Anne Foot.

Feb? 21st Was baptized Seth, son of Josiah & Hannah Crocker. ——

March 20th Was baptized Ebenezer, son of Ebenezer West. — — —

April 24th Was baptized Experience, child of Cornelius Bassett Sen? also William, son of Eli Bradley, and Charles-Backus, son of Alvan and Lucy Hyde.

May 8th Was baptized Fanny and Amanda, children of Levi Robinson.

June 5th Was baptized Betsey, daughter of Elizabeth Bennett. ——

June 7th Was baptized Lydia Barlow. wife of Peleg Barlow, at her own house, being unable to attend meeting. — — —

July 1(th Were baptized Hannah, daughter of Thomas Ewer, Huldah, daughter of Aaron Benedict, and Samuel-Crocker, son of David Baker.

Aug! 28th Was baptized Hope Davis, son of Nathan Davis. — — —

Sept 25th Were baptized Josiah, son of Josiah Yale, and Daniel, son of Archelaus Chadwick. — — — —

October 23d Was baptized Mary, daughter of Stephen & Lydia Toby.

1797.

Jany 8th Was baptized Lyman, child of Mrs Anne Bradley of Milton in the State of New-York. ——

Jany 15th Was baptized Lydia Bradley, daughter of Jesse Bradley Junr

Jany 22d Was baptized Josiah, son of Ebenezer Jenkins Junr

March 5th Was baptized Isaac, son of Nathl and Bethiah Bassett.

March 12th Was baptized Samuel Leonard Junr — and at the same time, he covenanted with this Church. ——

April 4th Thomas Crocker, an infant child of Mr Josiah Crocker, was baptized at the house of its father, on account of its being thought dangerously sick. ——

April 16th — Lewis, son of Samuel Davis was baptized. —— ——

April 30th Sally, child of Mr John & Joanna Gifford was baptized.

June 18th Joseph, son of Joseph & Martha Crocker, was baptized.

July 30th Josiah Willoughby was baptized, an adult. ——

July 30th Elizabeth, daughter of David Ingersol, was baptized.

Augt 13th Eunice, daughter of Mr Daniel & Mrs Elizabeth West, was baptized.

Augt 27th Polly & Lydia, children of Josiah Willoughby, were baptized.

Octr 30th Moses, son of Moses Ingersol, and John, son of Samuel Winegar, were baptized.

Decr 24th Rhoda, daughter of Jared Ingersol, was baptized. ——

1798.

Jany 7th Heman, son of Mr Oliver Hatch of Granville, who removed from this church, was baptized. —— —— ——

Jany 14th Sally, daughter of Mr Seth Nye, and Lydia, daughter of Mrs Hannah Remele, were baptized. - -

Feby 19th Isaac, son of Elisha & Mary Grant, and Charles, son of Paul & Susannah Ewer, were baptized

March 11th Abraham, son of Abraham & Tempe Perry, was baptized.

April 22d Nabby, daughter of Mr John & Mrs Ruth Parcival. — Palmira, daughter of Squire Stone, and Harriot, daughter of Alvan and Lucy Hyde, were all baptized. ——

May 14th Betsey-Crosby, daughter of Josiah & Hannah Crocker, was baptized.

May 20th James, son of James & Sarah Gifford, was baptized. ——

June 17th Mehitabel, daughter of Ebenezer & Mehitabel West, was baptized. —— ——

July 8th Joseph-Warren, son of Reuben and Nabby Barlow, was baptized. —— ——

Augt 5th Lyman, son of Asahel & Anne Foot, was baptized. ——

Sepr 9th Senah (alias Asenath) child of Huldah Finney, wife of Abraham Finney, was baptized.

Octor 1st   Philena, daughter of Jedediah & Sarah Crocker, and Eli, son of Eli and Phebe Bradley, were baptized.   ——   ——

Octor 7th   Harriot-Maria, daughter of Gideon & Olive Thompson, was baptized.

Octor 14th   Eunice, daughter of Mr̄ Prudence Ingersol, & Parmelia, daughter of Mr Joseph Bradley, were baptized.

Novr 4th   Ebenezer, son of Ebenezer Jenkins Junr , was baptized.

1799.

Jany 7th   Daniel, son of Jesse & Mamre Bartholomew, was baptized.

March 3d   Seth, son of Lemuel Barlow & Thankful his wife.

March 10th   Semantha, child of Josiah Willoughby.   ——

April 7th   John, son of David Baker, and Elizabeth, daughter of Samuel and Tabitha Winegar.

April 14th   Lydia, daughter of Abraham and Sarah Hall.

May 19th   Alva, son of Paul and Susannah Ewer.

June 23d   James, son of William and Marcy Ingersoll.

June 30th   Esther Bailey, wife of Thomas Bailey.

July 14th   Lucy, daughter of David and Sarah Ingersoll — also Smith, Orra, Wealthy and Thomas, children of Thomas and Esther Bailey.

July 28th   Anne Parcival — also Polly Turner, an adopted child of Mr Ebenezer & Mrs Mehitabel West — also, Reuben, John, Benjamin, Electa, Esther, Grace, Jared and Henry, children of Henry and Chloe Wansey.

Sepr 8th   Rachel, daughter of Cornelius & Remember Bassett — also, Marcy, daughter of Nathan and Lucy Davis.

Sepr 15th   Joseph, son of Nathanl & Bethiah Bassett.

Sepr 29th   Cornelius, son of Cornelius & Abigail Bassett. — also Lucy, daughter of Jesse Bradley Junr   ——

Octor 13th   Chloe, daughter of Henry & Chloe Wansey.

Novr 3d   Josiah, son of Josiah & Hannah Crocker.   ——

Novr 10th   Abigail, daughter of Asahel & Abigail Bradley.

Novr 19th   William, son of Squire Stone, was baptized at his father's house, by reason of the sickness and confinement of Mrs Stone.   ——

Novr 20th   John, son of James & Achsah Austin.

Decr 8th   Ebenezer-Cook & Elisha, children of Stephen & Lydia Bradley.

1800.

Jany 12th   Lucy Crocker, wife of Elisha Crocker, — also Phebe, Amanda, & Tirza, children of Samuel & Hannah Couch.

March 9th   Lydia Bradley, wife of Stephen Bradley, — Sarah Stewart — Sophia Crocker, Lemira Crocker, & Laura Crocker, all adults.   ——

April 27th   William, Electa-Lewis, John-Dimick, Lucy and Lucius, children of Elisha & Lucy Crocker.

May 1st   Stephen, son of Alvan & Lucy Hyde.

May 4th   Lydia Stanton, an adult -- also, William, son of Joseph and Martha Crocker —also, Hannah, daughter of John & Hannah Remele.

June 1st   Electa, daughter of Daniel and Lydia Wilcox.

June 8th   Charles, son of Asahel and Anne Foot.

July 6th   Lewis, son of John Gifford and Lyman, son of James and Sarah Gifford.

Aug! 3d   Thankful and Elias, children of Elias and Thankful Humphrey.

Aug! 17th   Abraham Finney, son of Abraham and Huldah Finney.

Aug! 24th   Asher, son of Jared Ingersoll.   ———

Aug! 31st   Benjamin, son of Ebenr & Mehitabel West.

Sep! 7th   Mabel & John, children of John and Prudence Couch.

Octor 19th   Sally Barlow was baptized.

Octor 26th   Lydia, daughter of Ebenr and Lydia Jenkins, was baptized.

Novr 9th   Aurelia, daughter of Jedidiah Crocker, was baptizel.

An account of persons married by the Rev.[d] Alvan Hyde.

July 19th 1792. Jonathan Wally and Mary Winslow were married.
August 23d Ebenezer Jenkins Jun.[r] and Lydia Smith were married.
October 18th Josiah Willoughby and Sally Backus were married.
Nov.[r] 20th Joshua Nye and Charity Parker were married. ——
Nov.[r] 29th Heman Bradley and Anne West were married. ——

1793.

Jan.[y] 17th Wally Backus and Grace Vandusen were married. ——
Jan.[y] 31st Ichabod Lathrop & Esther Pixley were married. ——
April 11th Ancel Bassett and Hannah Dimmuck were married.
Aug.[t] 21st Asael Foot and Anne Abbot were married. ——
October 17th Joseph Whiton to Amanda Garfield. ——
October 17th Jabez Bursley to Abigail Perry. —— ——
November 28th Pardon Austin to Rhoda Stanton. —— ——

1794.

March 27th Jacob Penoyer to Alice Hoyt Crocker. —— ——
May 25th Ephraim Sheldon to Lydia Gifford. —— ——
June 30th Silas Easton to Rachel Nye. —— ——
July 8th Isaac Barlow to Sally Casey.
August 24th John Read to Elizabeth Crocker. ——
October 8th David Hamlin to Sally Backus.
October 12th Samuel Hodges to Lydia Bradley. ——
October 19th Daniel Wilcox to Lydia Ball. —— ——
October 24th Stephen Dexter to Lydia Backus. —— ——
October 30th Ebenezer Hawes to Electa Northrop. ——
November 19th Joseph Hinckley to Polly Stewart. ——
November 20th Abraham Finney to Huldah Gifford. ——

1795.

Abijah Crosby to Caty Olds, Jan.[y] 15th——
Jan.[y] 15th Josiah Crocker to Hannah Crosby. ——
Feb.[y] 19th Benjamin Hamblin to Thankful Barlow. ——
Feb.[y] 19th Lemi Bradley to Ruth Newel of Lenox. ——
June 3d. Reuben Pixley Jun.[r] to Polly Chase.—— —
Sept. 7th Hope Davis to Mrs Lucy Bullard. ——
Sept. 10th William Sturges to Sallome Dimmuck.——

1796.

Jan.[y] 20th Sherman to Avis Collins. —— ——
Feb.[y] 18th Mr Paul Ewer to Miss Susannah Hamblin.—
March 10th Benjamin Adams to Sarah Parker.——
March 29th Reuben Penoyer to Polly Gifford.
April 19th John Remele to Hannah Barlow.
June 29th Nathaniel Hudson to Nabby Hinkley.

Octor 16th   Jacob Winegar to Anne Parker, ——   —

Novr 8th   Simeon Wright to Sukey Abbott.   ··—

Decr 15th   Ozias Judd to Lucena Hewlet.   —   —

Decr 25th   Harvey Osborn to Caty Gifford.—

1797.

Jany 12th   Samuel Winegar to Tabitha Crocker. —

Jauy 12th   Nathan Bassett to Azubah Jones.

Jany 14th   Joshua Howe to Urania Stevens.

Jany 18th   Peleg Barlow to Esther Griffin. —

Jany 22d   Lewis Gifford to Betsy Backus. —

Jany 26th   Ephraim Williams to Jemima Wormer.

June 29th   Nathan Ball Junr to Fear Chadwick. ——

June 29th   Zina Hinkley to Betsey Ball. —

Octor 4th   Jeremiah Vallet and Abiah Moot. — —

Octr 19th   Job Northrop to Sally Bennet.

Novr 9th   William Foot of Stockbridge to Abia Vollet.

Novr 23d   Daniel Parker to Anne Handy. —

Decr 28th   Joseph Frary of Becket to Sally Gifford. —   —

1798.

Jany 3d   William Bradley to Tabitha Hamblin. —

Feby 1st   Calvin Davis to Hannah Crocker. ——

June 21st   Elisha Dodge to Betsey Crosby. — —

✓Decr 15th   John White to Fear Perry.

Decr 20th   Oliver Wedge to Martha Grant.

1799.

Jany 3d   Elisha Kilburn to Lydia Tooley. ——

March 21st   Andrew Howk to Betsey Mansfield.

May 12th   Luther Day to Meribah Smith.

Sepr 16th   Thomas Chadwick to Lucinda Ingersoll.

Sepr 22d   John Gardner to Delia Childs. — —

1800.

Jany 26th   Simeon Clark to Lucy Backus.

Feby 6th   Eli Church to Elizabeth Chadwick.

April 24th   Jeduthan West to Phebe Wilcox. —

May 1st   Samuel Barlow to Sena Wilcox.

June 26th   John Rathbone to Celah Tobey. ——

Augt 8th   Cornelius Fessenden to Nancy Ball.

Sepr 1st   Philip Packard to Rachel Gifford.

Octor 6th   Asahel Stanton to Patty Ball.

Octr 30th   Amasa Porter to Betsey Winegar.

Octr 30th   Job Childs to Rhoda Hatch.

Octr 30th   Thomas Backus to Rebecca Couch.

Decr 18th   James Whiton to Deborah Webb Bassett.

An account of the Deaths in Lee, since the ordination of Mr. Hyde. ——

1792.

June 28th 1792—Died Hannah Crocker.
Sept —An infant child of Mr Jonathan Foot Junr .
Novr 2d   Thomas Nye, son of Deacon Levi Nye.

1793.

Feby 15th   An infant child of Mrs Farrar.
March 16th   An infant child of Reuben Barlow.
April 5th   Parmelia, daughter of Thomas Beecher.
April 21st   A child of John Crosby Junr —
June 28th   A Child of John Hewlits.
July 23d   A Child of Joshua Nye.
Augt 26th   A Child of James Austin.
Novr 11th   A son of James Youngs.
Decr 4th   A Child of Laurence Vandusen.
Novr 13th   Deliverance Backus, wife of Ichabol Backus, wo died at
Falmouth.
Decr 5th.   A Child of Jabez Clark.

1794.

Jany 14th   Cornelius, son of Lemuel Barlow.
Feby 7th   A Child of George Bennett.
Feby 9th   A Child of John Hewlit.
March 3d   A Child of Paul Ewer.
March 13th   A Child of Levi G. Porter.
March 20th   A Child of Elisha Grant.
May 7th   Died Arthur Perry Aged 73.
June 30th   Jesse, son of John Gifford.
July 21st   Content Crocker, wife of Noah Crocker, 63.
Augt 22d   Samuel Graves, aged 76 years.
Octor 20th   An Infant child of James Austin.
Decr 10th   An Infant child of James Gifford. ——
Decr 16th   A child of Jesse Smith.

1795.

Jany 5th   Charles, son of Benjm Hinkley, aged 16 months.
Feby 16th   An infant child of Silas Easton. ——
Feby 23d   Hannah Davis, wife of Hope Davis, aged 64.
March 3d   An infant Child of Ebenr West.
March 3d   An infant Child of Caleb Chadwick.
March 18th   Marcy Ewer, wife of Paul Ewer æt. 39.
April 9th   An infant child of Mr Shaw.

April 10th Widow Abigail Crocker, in the 90th year of her age.
April 11th An infant son of John Gifford.
April 14th An infant child of Sam! Hodges. ——
April 16th An infant child of Nath! Toby. ——
April 18th Benjamin Backus, of a cancer, aged 60 years.
April 23d An infant child of Aaron Graham.
March. An infant child of Lodowick Gardner, of which I did not hear in season.
May 2d an Infant Child of John Crosby aged one week.
May 5th Molly Casey, aged 24 years, who was eminent for her piety. *
June 5th Rhoda, daughter of Levi G. Porter, aged 3 years.
Sepr 9th Marcy Crocker, daughter of Joseph Crocker Junr aged 3 years and nine months.
Sepr 17th Died Mr Jonathan West, aged 58 years. —— ——
Septr 17th Died a daughter of Mr Jonathan Graves, aged 2 years.
Novr 10th Died Polly, daughter of Mr Elisha Grant, aged 2 years.
Nov. 19th Died Mrs Eunice Ingersol, wife of Mr Moses Ingersol, in the 51st year of her age.

1796.

Jany 8th Died Mr Joseph Crocker, son of Capt Thomas Crocker, in the 30.h year of his age.
Jany 19th Died an infant son of Mr Silas Clark.
Feby 11th Died an infant son of Mr John Keep.
Feby 20th Died Mrs Elizabeth Keep, wife of Mr John Keep, in the 40th year of her age.
March 6th Died Charles, son of Capt John Nye, aged 2 Months.
March 7th Died Kimball Porter son of Mr Sam! Porter, aged one year & 3 months. ——
April 23d Died Richard Whitney, son of Mr Wm Whitney, aged one year & 2 months.
May 1st An infant child of Mr James Gifford. —— ——
May 4th Died Mrs Anner Basset, wife of Mr Nathan Bassett, in the 41st year of her age.
May 13th Died Joseph Jones of Sandwich, in a fit of drunkenness, at the house of Mr Wilcox, being as was supposed about 47 years of age.
May 16th Died Henry Atkins, in the 70th year of his age.
July 5th Died Capt Thomas Crocker, in the 62d year of his age. ——
July 24th Died Joseph Crocker, son of Joseph Crocker Junr and grandson of Capt Thomas Crocker, aged about 8 months. —— ——
July 27th Died Abigail Swift, wife of Ebenezer Swift, aged 56.
Augt 7th Died Orra Blackman, son of James Blackman, aged one year, & 11 months.
Augt 11th Died Mrs Lydia Barlow, wife of Mr Peleg Barlow, aged 31 years. ——

Aug! 24th   Died Mrs Lydia Ewer, aged 74 years.

Sept 29th   Died an infant Child of Mr Reuben Barlow, aged 12 hours.—

Octor 15th   Died John, son of Mr John Hewlit, aged

1797.

Jany 2d   Died a daughter of Mr Seth Burden, aged 5 years.   — —

Jany 21st   Died Mrs   Hewlit, the wife of Mr John Hewlit, aged 33 years.   ———

Feby 16th   Died Peggy Casey, in the 16th year of her age.

Feby 25th   Died Ebenezer Chadwick Junr in the 25th year of his age.—

March 8th   Lied an infant child of Mr Wm Freeman, aged 2 weeks. —

April 1st   An infant child of Mr Jacob Winegar.   ———   ———

April 6th   An infant son of Mr Josiah Crocker, aged 10 days.

May 26th   An infant child of Mr Ancel and Mrs Hannah Bassett, aged 3 weeks.   ———

June 25th   Died Mrs Christene Gardner, wife of Mr Lodowick Gardner, aged 23 years.   ———

July 30th   1797— Died Mr Eleazer Turner, in the 30th year of his age.

Aug! 31st   Died, widow Silence Chase, in the 76th year of her age.

Septr 23d   An infant child of the widow Turner, aged 5 months.

Octr 23!   A son of Cornelius Hamblin, aged 17 months.

Decr 19th   Died, Mrs Desire Perry, wife of Mr David Perry, in ye 66th year of her age.   ———

Decr 29th   Died, Mr Nathan Ball, in the 62d year of his age.   ———

1798.

Jany 19th   Died Harriot Bassett, daughter of Mr Cornelius Bassett Junr , aged 2 years.

March 14th   Died Mr John Winegar, aged 55 years. In the 29th year of his age, he was severely frozen; being left in the woods, and without shelter. Both of his feet came off, and his constitution was so injured, that he never had good health afterwards.

May 2!   Died Mr Benjamin Hamblin aged 67 years.

May 3d   Died an infant child of Mr James Austin, aged but a few hours.   ———   ———   ———

May 6th   Died Dennis Casey, of a consumption, aged 20 years.   — —

June 5th   Died Anner Bassett, of a consumption, aged 18 years.   ——

June 13th   Died Catharina Winegar, of a consumption, aged 33 years. She was an example of piety in her life, and met death with fortitude & composure.   ———

July 28th   Died at Mr Wm Sturges, Cynthia Chadwick, aged 13 years.

Sepr 2d   Died Zeruiah Crocker, of a consumption, aged 20 years.   — —

Nov. 30th   Died Widow Dorcas Crocker, in the 79th year of her age.

Decr 23d   Died Betsey C. Crocker, aged 9 months.

1799.

Jany 3d Died Roxana Howk, daughter of Mr Abr^m Howk, in the fourth year of her age.

Jany 7th Died, Mrs Sarah Graves, wife of Mr Phineas Graves.

Feby 7th Died Miss Remember Toby, daughter of Stephen Toby, in the 22d year of her age. ———

Feby 21st Died Mrs Elizabeth Turner, widow of Mr Eleazer Turner, aged 39 years.

March 8th Died Mr Daniel Church, aged 92 years, wanting a few days.

March 11th Died Mrs Meribah Burden, the wife of Mr Timothy Burden, aged,

March 13th Died an infant child of Mr Stephen Tobey. ———

April 3d Died Mrs Lydia Toby, the wife of Mr Stephen Toby, in the 43d year of her age.

June 1st Died Mrs Sarah Couch wife of Mr John Couch, in the 77th year of her age.

June 8th Died a son of Mr John Couch Junr aged one year & nine months.

June 29th Died Bulah, daughter of Mr Elijah Peet aged 9 years. ———

July 19th Died Laurence Vandusen, in the 32d year of his age.

July 20th Died a child of Mr Polly, aged one year and seven months.

Aug! 5th An infant child of Mr Alvan Foot, aged but a few hours.

Aug! 9 h Died Mr Thomas Northrop, aged 72 years. ——— ———

Aug! 18th Samuel Couch, son of Mr Samuel Couch, aged 15 months.

Sepr 6th Died a twin child of Mr Polly, aged about one year & 9 months.

Sepr 21st Died, Mary Ann Wormer, daughter of Mr Aaron Wormer, in the 8th year of her age.

Octor 5th Died a child of Capt John Stearns, aged one year and 6 months.

Decr 21st Died Moses Ramsdale, son of Mr Jehu Ramsdale, aged 7 years. ——— ———

Decr 23d An infant child of Mr Andrew Howk.

1800.

Feby 22d Died Miss Lucinda Ingersoll, daughter of Wm Ingersoll Esqr in the 36th year of her age.

March 21st Died Mrs Elizabeth West, aged 88 years.

April 9th Died Mr Daniel Church, in the 60th year of his age.

May 16th Died Electa Wilcox, in the 29th year of her age.

May 27th An infant child of Mr Elijah West.

Aug! 10 h Died Joseph Bassett, son of Mr Nath! Bassett, aged one year.

Sept 30th Died Achsah Taylor, wife of William Taylor, in the 24th year of her age.

Novr 9th Died Miriam Hatch, wife of Josiah Hatch, aged 88 years.

Inscriptions from the Cemeteries.

In the old grave-yard, now in the north-east corner of the cemetery near the center of the town, there are 72 monuments with memorials to 84 persons who died before 1801. Mattey, daughter of Joseph and Lois Hendy (see p. 85,) is supposed to have been the first person buried there. Doubtless there were earlier deaths among the settlers here, but no certain record of any has been found. In Holland's Hist. of Western Mass. (vol. 2, p. 516,) is the following: "The first death that occurred in Lee befell a child of John Winegar. The death occurred at Crow Hollow, and the child was buried on the West side of the river." Probably the statement was made on traditional authority.

It is supposed one of the earliest graves is marked by a rough stone bearing only the rudely carved letters S B. The name for which these letters stand has not been determined. The stone with the letters I V D, marks the grave of Isaac VanDeusen, 8 years old, a son of Matthew VanDeusen.

Only two dated before 1801 are in the South Lee cemetery; one at the grave of Isaac Davis, the first settler, the other at the grave Abijah Stearns.

A few early graves in each cemetery are marked with uninscribed, unhewn slabs of stone. There are, also, several early graves marked in the same manner near the residence of C. E. Morley, Cape St., where, according to tradition, some of the settlers in that section named Gifford and Roberts were buried.

If any of the early inhabitants were buried elsewhere in town, all knowledge of their graves is lost.

Owing to weathering, probably some of the punctuation has been effaced from some of the stones.

The interlined letters and words in the inscriptions here given, are shown as well as possible with ordinary type. On the stones they are close to the lines to which they belong.

Joſeph F. ſon of Mr
James & Mrs Achſa
Auſtin. died May, 16
1791, aged 12 Month
Alſo Zeſna; thir ſon
died Auguſt, 26th
1793, aged 18 Month
*Margaret their dau'tr
died at ſalem ſtate of
N york Oct 21 1786,
aged 3 Months.*

An Infant Son of
Mr James & Mrs:
Achsah Austin
who was Still bor
Oct 20 1794

In memory of Zaf-
na ſon of Mr Jame
& Mrs Achſah
Auſtin died April
16 1797 aged 18M
Alſo their ſon was
born & died May
3d 1798

Sarah, daughtr of
Mr. Nathan &
Mrs. Ruhamah
Ball. died Augu
1 1784 aged
11 Years & 3 Mo

Annah Bassett,
was born
June 12, 1780.
and died June
5, 1798. aged
18 years.

In Memory of
Joseph Bafsett fon
to Mr Nathaniel &
Mrs Bethiah Bafs-
ett who died Au
gust 10th 1800
aged one year &
3 days

In memory of
Harriot Dautr to
Mr Cornelius junr &
Mrs Abigail Baf-
sett who died Jany
19th 1798 aged 2
years & 9 days

Phebe Died August 30th 1777
Aged 1 year & 9 Months.
Thomas Died February 17th
1788 Aged 14 Months.
Permela Died April 3d 1793
Aged 2 years & 3 Months.
Children of Mr. Thomas &
Mrs Phebe Beecher.

Nancy, dautr of Mr.
Cornelius Bafsett Jun
by Mrs Abigail his
wife. died with the
Small pox March
19th, 1785, aged 12
Months & 19 days.

Betfey (dautr of
Mr. Gerge & Mrs
Elifabeth) Benne
died Sept 7th 1790
aged 5 Months.

Mrs Defire Chadwi^{ck}
the late Confort of
Mr Abiathar Chad
wick died Auguft
13th 1790 in the 35th
year of her age
_____
No age nor sex can
   Death defy
Think Mortals what
   it is to die

In memory of Miss Ze-
ruiah Crocker who died
Sep 2nd 1798 in the 21ft
year of her age
Tis long since death had
the majority Yet strange:
the living lay not to heart

In Memory of Mrs
Content, the late
Confort of Mr Noa^h
Crocker, who Died
July 23d. 1794 in
the 65th year
of her age.

Mrs. H a n n a h D a v i s
the wife of M r. Hope
Davis Died February 23^d
1795 i n the 65th year
of her age
_____
How sudden was the stro^{ke}
When the Almighty spoke
My Friends & Children
   now draw near
And fee that you for
   Death prepare

Mercy Hambliⁿ
Crocker Died
Sep! 8th 1795,
in the 4thyear
of her age.
The above were the Children
of Infign Joseph & Mary Crocker

Joseph Crocke^r
jun^r Died July
24th 1796,
aged 7 Month^s
& 6 Days.

The blooming cheeks, the lovely charms,
Lie clasped in Deaths cold Icy arms.

Polly Daut^r of M^r
Silas & Mrs Rachel
Eaftoa died February
15th 1795 aged 16 days.

Mrs Marcy Ewer the
wife of Mr Paul Ewer
died March 18th 1795 in
the 39th year of her age
Farewell my friends
dry up your tears
Here sleeps my dust
till Christ appears

In memory of an
Infant son to Mr
Alvan & Mrs Sally
FOOT who died
August 5th 1799
aged 9 hours

Ye active babes & childre n
all
Behold the scene of
childrens fall
My day was short my
hours few
And bid this world &
all adieu

David (son of
Mr. David &
Mrs. Elizabeth)
Foot) died Oct.
14th, 1790, age d
3 Months.
Sleep on my babe
and take your reft
God calls you
home
He saw it best.

Jared died | Eunis died
May 15th 1785 March 19th
aged 2 Years 1794 aged
& 8 Month 3 Years.
The heirs of Mr.
Elish & Mrs. Mary gran

Thomas, son of
Mr Elisha & Mr.
Elizabeth Free-
man. died June
28th 1780 aged
3 years.
The God that • • •
[Stone broken.]

Nancy Daut r of
Mr Mofes & Mrs
Relie Hall who
Died February 19th
1797 aged 16 days

William Phinney
Hamblin Son to
Mr Cornelius & M^{rs}
Marcy Hamblin
died October 23d
1797 aged 1 year 4
Months & 15 days

Rochana Daut^r of
Mr Abraham &
Mrs Easther Hook
who died January
3^d 1799 in the _th
year of her age

In Memory of Mrs
Mariam Hatch wife
to Mr Jofiah Hatch
who died Nov^m
9th 1800 aged
83 years

In Memory of Charles
son to Mr Benjamin &
Mrs Puella Hinckley
who died Jany 5th
1795 aged 16 months
& 20 days

Leua, Daut^r to M^r
Samuel, & M^{rs} Ly-
dia Hodges, died
April 14, 1795
aged 2 months.

Sacred to the memory
of Mrs Eunice Ingerfoll
Confort of Mr Mofes Ingerfoll who departed thi^s
life Nov 19 1795 in the
51ft year of her age.

Surviving friends altho you mo^{rn}
Let this confole I fhall return
The righteous Judge can by his ^{word}
Bring me triumphing with
the Lord

In memory of Mrs Elifa-
beth Jenkins Confort of
Mr Ebenzer Jenkins (late of
Barnftable deceafed) who died
Octr 28th 1788 age l 91 years

Behold my friends while pafing ^{by}
This ftone informs you where I lie
Tho I have lived to ninty one
Yet you may die while you are
young

Here lies
Worthy to be lamented
Mrs SIBYL HURD
Wife of
STEPHEN LEONARD
who departed this life
July 19th 1787
in the 24th Year
of her Age.

My glafs is run my Grave you see,
Prepare for Death and follow me.

Stephen Leon
ard junr died
May 1787

In memory of
Thomas Nye fon
to Deacon Levy
& Mrs Sarah Nye
who Died Nov
2nd 1792 in the
19thyear of his age

In memory of an
Infant, dau^{tr} of Mr.
Joshua & Mrs.
Charity Nye. who
died July 23^{d} 1793
aged 5 days.

Hulda^{h} the dau-
ghter of Mr. Le-
vi & Mrs Catharin^{e}
Porter, died Marc^{h}
13 1794 aged 8
yeas^{r} & 13 days.

Rhoda daut^{r} to Mr
Levi & Mrs Catharin^{e}
Porter died June 5th
1795 in the 4th year
of her age.

In memory of Mrs Lydia
Tobey confort to Mr Ste
phen Tobey who died
April 3d 1799 in the
43d year of her age.

Gods people are made willing
in the day of his Power

In memory of Mifs Re-
member Tobey: Daut.ʳ to
Mr Stephen,&Mrs Lydia
Tobey: who died Feb. 6th
1799. in the 22 year of
her age.

The blooming cheeks the lovely ch ᵃʳᵐˢ
Lie clasp'd in Deths cold icy arms

This ftone was Erected
by Seth Backus junʳ

In Memory of
Mrs
Lucy, wife of Mr.
John Williams,
who Departed
this Life, Aug. 28,
AD. 1786: Æ. 24.

Farewell my loving wife,
We bid a short Adieu,
You can not come to me again
But I must come to you.

Mary Dauᵗʳ of Mʳ
William & Mʳˢ Sarah
Whitney Died July 27ᵗʰ
1790 aged 1 Month

Inscriptions indistinct in the photo-engravings, pp. 85—91.

In Memory of
Mr. Arthur Perry
who died May 7,
1794 in the 73d
year of his age.

*Adieu my fpoufe my
children dear
I leave this world of* ᵖᵃⁱⁿ
*Let virtue be your
Practice here
' we do meet a*

Page 85.

M   RS
Rebecca, wife
of Mʳ Oliver Hat ᶜʰ
died May 1ˢᵗ 1788
in the 3ᵈ year
of her age.

*Farewell my friends
dry up your tears,
My dust lies here
Till Christ appears.*

Page 87.

On stone to the memory of Esther and Lydia Bradley ;—see p. 87:

*Decaying mortals
here's the place
The houfe deftin'd
for Adams race
Be ready then
to meet the Lamb
Of God. the Judge.
the Great I AM.*

This ftone erected by Row
land THATCHER jun^r to
perpetuate the memory of
Mifs Electa WILCOX who
departed this Life May 16th
1800 Aged 19 years 2 month
& 14 days.

All you that ftop my tomb to fee
As I am here so you muft be,
Repent, repent now you have time,
For I was taken in my prime.

Page 87.

On stone erected to the children of Jonathan Foot Jr. ;—ee p. 87:

*Thofe guiltlefs charmes, those
marks of genius are surprest,
Which nurst the fondeft hopes
in tender parents breafts.*

In memory of Mr

JOHN WIEGAR

who Departed this
Life the 14th of
March 1 7 9 8
Aged 55 years & 2 Mo

In folemn filence here I lie
Pray from me learn that you must die
All youthful fcenes of pleafure bright
Muft end as watches of the night

O may this be your happy case
That he who gives you length of days
May raise you to His corts above
There to pertake of boundlefs love

Page 80.

Two infants of Jaco
& Anna Winegars
One died March
3 1797 The oth-
er died June 16
1802

Page 80.

In Memory of Mrs Mary
Bafsett the late Confort of
Mr Nathan Bafsett who Died
May 4th 1796 in the 44th
year of her Age.

Death is a debt to Nature due,
Which I have paid & so muft you,
Here let me reft my weary head,
Till Chrift my Lord fhall rais
           the Dead,

Page 91.

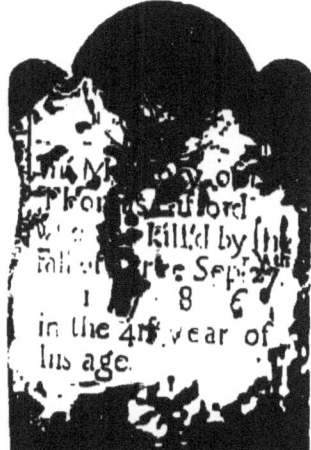

In Memory of
Thomas Clifford
who was kill'd by the
fall of a tree Sept 27
1 8 6
in the 41st year of
his age.

In Memory of Mr
Elmer ...
... Bradly who
died ...
...
...
... kill'd by
... 73 ...

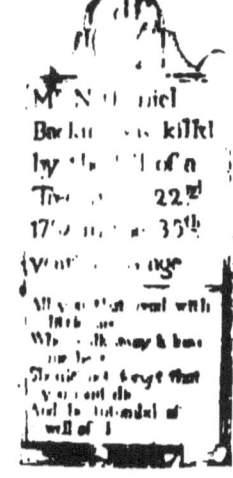

Mr Nathaniel
Backus was kill'd
by the fall of a
Tree ... 22d
17.. in the 35th
year of his age

All you that read with
little care
Who walk away & leave
me here
Don't you forget that
you must die
And be intombed as
well as I

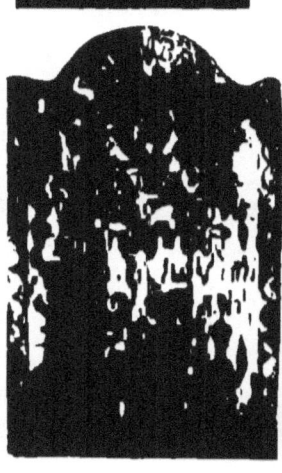

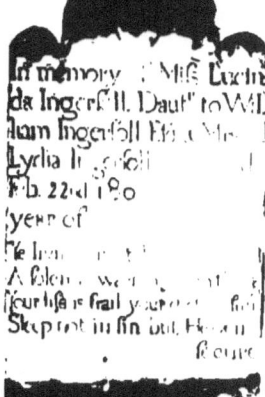

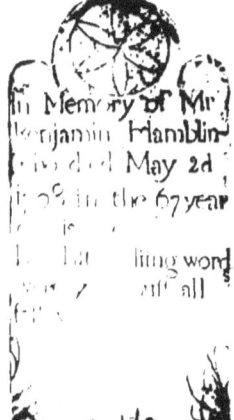

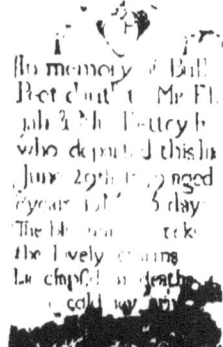

Appendix.

First Publishment on page 1.

The following from Holland's History of Western Mass. vol. 2, p. 516, completes the mutilated record on p. 1 of this vol. :—

"The first 'publishment' of intentions of marriage, recorded on the town books, perpetuates the names of Noah Burdin of Lee and Avis Their of Chesterfield."

Marriages of Residents of Lee recorded in other Towns.

In a volume in the custody of the Town Clerk of Monterey containing a transcript of the records of Marriages by Rev. Alonijah Bidwell and Rev. Joseph Avery, the first two pastors of the church in Tyringham, are the following :—

Solemnized by Rev. A. Bidwell.

1778 June 4th Capt Abijah Merrill & Hannah Chadwick

1779 June 30th John Sterns & Luce Merrill

1782 Jany 10 Freeman Mosier & Hepzibah Orton

1782 Oct 17th Jonathan Graves & Anna Taylor

Solemnized by Rev. Joseph Avery.

1790 May 26th Reuben Davis of Lee & Polly Abbott of Tyringham

1790 Nov 11th Timothy Aldin of Tyringham & Lowis Wilcocks of Lee

1791 Jany 27th Stephen Markham of Tyringham & Dolly Jackslin of Lee

1791 July 7th Reuben Marsh of Lee & Lydia Rathbun, of Tyringham.

1791 October 12th Artemas Rogers of Lee, & Phebe Cross, do [Lee]

1792 June 21st Jonathan Foot of Lee, & Temperance Holly, of G Barrington

—From the Lenox Records:—
By William Walker, J. P.,

Ephraim Hollister of Lee to Laurana Canfield of Lenox, 15th Decr 1785—

T. B. (Orig.) p. 347,

John Briggs to Martha Gibbs both of Lee on the 1st of Jany 1789. —

Do. p. 337.

By Eldad Lewis, J. P.,

David Hayward of Lee & Mercy Howland of Lenox, Feby 10th 1795.

Do. p. 339.

Also the following "Intentions":

1790, May 31, Intentions of Marriage Legally published and certified between Jonathan Keith of Lenox & Polly Backous of Lee

Do. p. 301.

— From the Stockbridge Records:—

David Ingersoll and Sarah Parsons were married Dec 13th 1781 by Rev. Stephen West.

—From 1st Book of Records, Cong. church, Pittsfield: —
By Rev. Thomas Allen.

1795, Dec. 24. Mr Silas Stephens of Lee & Miss Irene Tracy of Pitts! were married——

—Under "Marriages" in a published vol. of vital records of Sharon, Ct., by Lawrence Van Alstine:—

Elisha Collins of Lee and Lovina Gates of Sharon, Mar. 20, 1785. m. by Ebenezer Knibloe, 1st Pastor of S. Amenia [N. Y.] Church.

Abraham Perry of Lee and Temperance Hatch of Sharon, m. Feb. 24, 1788.

Births omitted from the Records pp. 12-42.

Children of David Ingersoll & Sarah his Wife (See p. 85.)

William & Alvan — born Dec 22d. 1801 (Twins)
Elihu Parons — " Sepr. 20. 1804.

Children of Wm Perry and Content his wife

Fear born	Feb. 20 - 1777 —	Ruth	Novr 14th 1783 —
Hannah —	21 - 1778	Sarah	July 28 — 1784
Phebe	March 22 1780	John	August 1 — 1788 —
Lucy	July 28 1781		

Children of Joel Putnam & Elizabeth

Sarah Maria Johnson (Becket) Jany 30. 1848 —		Sally Putman (Becket) March 10. 1800
Lorinna	"	"	March 23 1.03	Abner	do — do	June 18 1802
Caroline	"	"	Feb 14. 18.0	Joel	do	do	Nov 10. 1804
James Allen	Lee		Sep 14 1817	Ransom Nathan do		June 18 1805
Orson R			Apr 14. 1819	Sardis Barns	do	Jany 2. 1808
Julia Tryphena		"	July 27 1821	Lucy Anne	d	[?] oct 14. 18.3

The explanation of the above peculiar record is: Joel Putnam, a widower with five (or six) children, married Mrs. Elizabeth Johnson, with three children, and three children were born to them. The births, except two, are recorded as below in Becket, but there is no record there of the death of James Johnson, or of marriage between any of the parties.

Sally Putnam dau. Joel & Sally born Mar. 10, 1799
Abner " s. n " " " June 18, 1801
Joel " " " " " Dec. 10, 1803
Ransom " " " " " June 15, 1805
Sardis " " " " " Jan. 22, 18.7
Sally wife of Joel Putnam died June 10, 1813.
James Allin Putnam son of Joel & Elizabeth born Sept. 14, 1815
Orson Revallion " " " " " Oct. 14, 1819

Sally Maria Johnson dau. James & Elizabeth born Jan. 30, 1804
Lorana Eliza " " " " " Mar. 23, 180;
Caroline Content " " " " " Feb. 14, 18.0

Index.

BAPTISMS.

Bradley, Ebenezer Cook, 68.
    Eli, 68.
    Elisha, 68.
    Eunice, 66.
    Joel, 64.
    Josiah, 64.
    Lucy, 68.
    Lydia, 67.
    Lydia, 68.
    Lyman, 67.
    Parmelia, 68.
    Philo, 64.
    Polly, 64.
    Sally, 65.
    William, 66.
Bullard, Charlotte, 57.
Carpenter, Darius, 63.
Casey, Mary, 64.
Chadwick, Ancel, 65.
    Archelus, 56.
    Daniel, 66.
    Fear, 54.
    Heman, 54.
    John, 54.
    John, 55.
    Joseph, 54.
    Mary, 55.
    Ruth, 57.
    Samuel, 56.
    Sarah, 56.
Church, Anna, 57.
    Daniel, 55.
    Daniel, 65.
    Hannah, 56.
    Huldah, 64.
    James, 64.
    Polly, 64.
Coffey, Crecia, 54.
Couch, Amanda, 68.
    John, 69.
    Mabel, 69.
    Phebe, 68.
    Tirza, 68.
Crocker, Abigail, 65.
    Asa, 64.
    Aurelia, 69.
    Benjamin, 64.
    Betsey, 63.
    Betsey Clark, 64.
    Betsey Crosby, 67.
    Celah, 63.
    Electa, 63.
    Electa Lewis, 68.
    Elizabeth, 63.
    Elizabeth, 65.
    Grissilda, 64.

Crocker, Huggins, 63.
    Jedediah, 64.
    Jedediah Davis, 65.
    John Dimick, 68.
    Joseph, 65.
    Joseph, 67.
    Josiah, 68.
    Laura, 68.
    Lemira, 68.
    Lucius, 68.
    Lucy, 68.
    Lucy, 68.
    Noah, 65.
    Olive, 63.
    Philena, 68.
    Polly, 64.
    Polly, 66.
    Samuel, 54.
    Samuel, 65.
    Sally, 64.
    Sarah, 64.
    Sarah, 65.
    Seth, 66.
    Sophia, 68.
    Thomas, 67.
    William, 68.
    William, 69.
Davis, Bathsheba, 65.
    Charity Hall, 64.
    Elisha Parmele, 56.
    Hannah Crocker, 64.
    Hope, 66.
    Hopestill, 56.
    Isaac, 64.
    Lewis, 67.
    Lucy, 64.
    Lucy, 64.
    Mary, 56.
    Mercy, 68.
    Nathan, 64.
    Priscilla, 63.
    Samuel, 56.
    Samuel, child of, 57.
    Wait Hatch, 66.
Denio, Betsey, 65.
Dickinson, Daniel, 64.
    Miriam, 63.
Dodge, Asahel, 63.
    Hannah, 64.
    Heman, 63.
    Samuel Stanley, 63.
    Sarah, 63.
Ewer, Alva, 68.
    Ansel, 54.
    Asa, 65.
    Charles, 67.

Ewer, Ebenezer, 54.
    Eleazer, 57.
    Elisha, 54.
    Elizabeth, 57.
    Hannah, 66.
    Jane, 64.
    John Crocker, 64.
    Lydia, 54.
    Martha, 64.
    Mary, 54.
    Mary Bursley, 64.
    Mercy, 64.
    Nabby, 64.
    Paul. 66.
    Seth, 54.
    Thomas, 54.
    Tilson, 64.
Finney, Abraham, 69.
    Aseuath, 67.
    Ezra Thompson, 66.
Fish, Thankful, 54.
Foot, Asahel, 64.
    Charles, 69.
    Elizabeth, 66.
    John, 57.
    Jonathan, 56.
    Lyman, 67.
    Sarah Ann, 64.
    Sarah Ann, 65.
    Solomon, 64.
    William, 63.
Freeman, Charles, 64.
    Elisha, 63.
    Elizabeth, 63.
    Fanny, 63.
    Lydia Percival, 63.
    Thomas, 63.
Fuller, Elihu., 65.
    Jacob, 65.
    Lucy, 65.
    Thomas Williams, 65.
Garfield, Daniel, 65.
    Polly, 65.
    Silas, 65.
Gifford, Abigail, 57.
    Abraham, 57.
    Alvan, 65.
    Eunice, 65.
    Geneverah, 64.
    James, 65.
    James, 67.
    Jesse, 56.
    Jesse, 64.
    John, 64.
    John, 65.
    Lewis, 69.

Gifford, Lydia, 57.
    Lyman, 69.
    Phebe, 57.
    Ruth, 64.
    Sally, 67.
    Sylva, 64.
    Sylvanus, 64.
    Thomas, 57.
Goodspeed, Abigail, 49.
    Thankful, 49.
Grant, David, 55.
    Elisha, 54.
    Esther, 55.
    Eunice, 57.
    Isaac, 67.
    Jared, 54.
    Polly, 65.
    Prudence, 54.
    Ruth, 54.
    Thankful, 56.
Hall, Lydia, 68.
Hamblin, Nathaniel, 64.
    Tabitha, 65.
Handy, Elizabeth, 64.
Hatch, Alpheus, 63.
    Daniel Lewis, 56.
    David, 57.
    Eli, 56.
    Heman, 67.
    Justus, 63.
    Lemuel, 57.
    Oliver, 63.
    Polly, 64.
    Tabitha, 63.
    Tamar, 65.
    Thomas Davis, 63.
    Wait, 63.
Hinckley, Content, 64.
Hinsdale, Lydia, 65.
Hodges, Lucy, 66.
Humphrey, Elias, 69.
    Thankful, 69.
Hyde, Alvan, 65.
    Charles Backus, 66.
    Harriet, 67.
    Stephen, 68.
Ingersoll, Anna, 49.
    Asher, 69.
    Betsey, 49.
    Billy, 49.
    Cela, 63.
    David, 64.
    David, 66.
    Ebenezer Niblow, 64.
    Elenor, 49
    Elihu, 63.

Ingersoll, Elizabeth, 66.
   Elizabeth, 67.
   Eunice, 68.
   James, 68.
   John, 64.
   John Calvin, 49.
   Lois, 64.
   Lucretia, 56.
   Lucy, 68.
   Luther, 49.
   Lydia, 63.
   Merit, 64.
   Moses, 57.
   Moses, 67.
   Polly, 64.
   Reuben, 65.
   Rhoda, 67.
   Sarah, 63.
   Sarah, 66.
   Seth Crocker, 63.
   Sophia, 57.
   Theodore, 56.
   Thomas, 65.
   William, 63.
Jenkins, Ebenezer, 68.
   Henry William, 65.
   Josiah, 67.
   Lydia, 69.
   Nathan, 66,
Kellogg, Otis, 54.
King, Artemesia, 66.
Leonard, Samuel, 67.
Nye, Betsey, 57.
   Caleb, 56.
   Charity, 64.
   Charles, 66.
   Elisha, 54.
   Esther, 64.
   Hannah, 64.
   Ira, 64.
   John, 64.
   Joshua, 66.
   Lois, 64.
   Sally, 67.
   Sarah, 66.
   Seth, 55.
   Thankful, 57.
Penoyer, Truman, 49.
Percival, Anne, 68.
   Content, 66.
   Elisha, 63.
   Elisha, 64.
   Fear, 63.
   Hannah Gates, 65.
   Huldah, 63.
   James, 65.

Percival, John, 63.
   John, 64.
   John, 65.
   Montgomery, 65.
   Nabby, 67.
   Polly, 63.
   Ruth, 64.
   Ruth, 65.
   Samuel, 65.
Perry, Abraham, 67
   Arthur, 65.
   Dama, 65.
   Polly, 65.
Porter, Abigail, 65.
   Grace, 65.
   Kimball, 66.
   Lorain, 65.
   Lydia, 65.
   Mary, 65.
Remele, Hannah, 69.
   Lydia, 67.
Robinson, Amanda, 66.
   Fanny, 66.
Sheldon, Lydia, 66.
Stanton, Lydia, 69.
Stewart, Sarah, 68.
Stone, Palmira, 67.
   William, 68.
Taylor, Deborah, 64.
Thompson, Chauncey, 64.
   Harriet Maria, 68.
   Hezekiah Orton, 64.
   Olive, 65.
   Rhoda, 64.
Tilly, Hannah, 64.
   Leeta, 64.
   Lucy, 65.
   Rhoda, 64.
   Samuel, 64.
Tobey, Achsah, 65.
   Asael, 57.
   Celah, 55.
   Cynthia, 65.
   Deborah, 64.
   Deborah, 65.
   Lydia, 54.
   Lydia, 56.
   Mary, 65. Mary, 66
   Nathaniel, 56.
   Nathaniel, 64.
   Remembrance, 55.
   Samuel, 65.
   Sarah, 64.
   Stephen, 55.
Turner, Polly, 68.
Tuttle, James, 64.

Tyler, David, 65.
    Sally, 65.
    Sibyl, 65.
Wansey, Benjamin, 68.
    Chloe, 68.
    Electa, 68.
    Esther, 68.
    Grace, 68.
    Henry, 68.
    Jared, 68.
    John, 68.
    Reuben, 68.
West, Abigail, 63.
    Alvah, 66.
    Amy, 49.
    Benjamin, 69.
    Daniel, 54.
    Ebenezer, 66.
    Elizabeth, 54.
    Elizabeth, 56.
    Ephriam, 64.
    Ezekiel, 55.
    Eunice, 67.
    Hannah, 63.
    Heman, 49.
    Ira, 56.
    Joel, 64.
    Mehitabel, 67.
    Orson, 57.
    Lucy, 54

West, Pelatiah, 64.
    Phebe, 64.
    Prince, 56.
    Sally, 55.
    Saviah, 54.
    Stephen, 64.
    Thomas Tracy, 54.
    Timothy Nye, 64.
Wilcox, Daniel, 64.
    Electa, 49.
    Electa, 69.
    Hudson, 66.
Willoughby, Josiah, 67.
    Lydia, 67.
    Polly, 67.
    Semantha, 68.
Winegar, Electa, 56.
    Elizabeth, 68.
    John, 67.
    Stephen, 55.
Yale, Electa, 65.
    John, 57.
    Josiah, 66.
    Lucy Tracy, 63.
    Sirus, 56.
Youngs, Alvin, 57.
    Benjamin, 49.
    Ezra, 56.

Williams, Lucy, 56.

L. of C.

Santie, Betsey, 60.
    Daniel, 60.
Sheldon, Ephraim, 61.
Stanley, Jerusha. 53,54.
    Molly, 60.
Stanton, Lydia, 63.
Stewart, Sarah, 63.
Stone, Rebecca, 62.
    Squire, 62.
Squier, Adria, 63.
    Sally, 62.
Taylor, Deborah, 60.
Thatcher, Elizabeth, 62.
    Rowland, 62.
Thayer, Anne, 62.
    Nathaniel, 62.
Thompson, Olive, 60.
Tilley, Hannah, 60.
    Samuel, 60.
Tobey, Deborah, 60.
    Lydia, 53, 54.
    Nathaniel, 60.
Totman, Joseph, 50.
Tuttle, James, 60.
    Sarah, 60.
Tyler, Ruth, 60.
    Sarah, 61.

Wansey, Chloe, 62.
Wells, Zurviah, 60.
West, Daniel, 60.
    Ebenezer, 60.
    Elizabeth, 53.
    Elizabeth, 60.
    Mehitabel, 60.
    Mehitabel, 60.
    Oliver, 50, 54.
    Prince, 49, 50.
    Thankful, 50.
Wilcox, Daniel, 60.
    Peter, 60.
    Tabitha, 49, 52.
Willoughby, Josiah, 62.
Winegar, Elizabeth, 52.
    Huldah, 60.
    John, 63.
    Katharina, 53.
    Samuel, 60.
Wormer, Grace, 62.
    Jeremiah, 61.
Yale, Josiah, 56.
    Ruth, 56.
Youngs. Hannah, 51.
    James, 51.

Easton, Silas, 5, 70.
Eddy, Rachel, 3.
Ewer, Paul, 7, 70.
Fessenden, Cornelius, 10, 71.
    Lucy, 4.
Finney, Abraham, 5, 70.
    Deborah, 2.
Foot, Alvan, 9.
    Asahel, 4, 70.
    David, 3.
    Fenner, 2.
    Jonathan, 93.
    Sally, 5.
    Sarah, 1.
    William, 8, 71.
Fowler, Levi, 9.
Frary, Joseph, 8, 71.
Fuller, Amos, 1.
Gardner, Betsey, 9.
    Hannah, 9.
    John, 9, 71.
    Lodowick, 9.
Garfield, Amanda, 4, 70.
Gates, Lavina, 93.
Gibbs, Martha, 93.
Gifford, Abigail, 3.
    Caty, 7, 71.
    Huldah, 5, 70.
    Lewis, 7, 71.
    Lydia, 5, 70.
    Polly, 7, 70.
    Rachel, 10, 71.
    Sally, 8, 71.
    Sarah, 3.
    Sylvanus, 3.
Gillet, Nathaniel, 2.
Gleason, Nathaniel, 6.
Goodrich, Lois, 3.
Grant, Isaac, 3.
    Martha, 9, 71.
Graves, Jonathan, 93.
Green, John, 3.
Griffin, Esther, 8, 71.
Haas [Hoose], John, 2.
Hamblin, Bathiah, 2.
    Benjamin, 6, 70.
    Betsey, 3.
    David, 5, 70.
    Deliverance, 1.
    Martha, 3.
    Nabby, 10.
    Susanna, 7, 70.
    Tabitha, 8, 71.
    Thankful, 10.
Hancock, Jemima, 1.
Handy, Anne, 8, 71.

Hatch, Edward, 11.
    Lewis, 2.
    Rhoda, 11, 71.
    Temperance, 93.
Hawes, Ebenezer, 70.
Hayward, David, 93.
Hinckley, Joseph, 5, 70.
    Nabby, 7, 70.
    Zina, 8, 71.
Hodges, Samuel, 70.
Hollister, Ephraim, 93.
Holly, Temperance, 93.
Howard, Mehitabel, 3.
Howe, Joshua, 71.
Howk, Andrew, 9, 71.
    Ficha, 2.
Howland, Mercy, 93.
Hudson, Nathaniel, 7, 70.
Huggins, Anne, 1.
Hulet, John, 8.
    Lucena, 7, 71.
Huntington, Azel, 8.
Hyde, Alvan, 4.
Ingersoll, Calvin, 3.
    David, 93.
    Jared, 3.
    Lucinda, 10, 71.
    Luther, 9.
    Moses, 7.
    William, Jr., 3.
Jackslin, Dolly, 93.
Jenkins, Ebenezer, Jr., 4, 70.
Johnston, Stephen, 6.
Jones, Azuba, 8, 71.
Judd, Ozias, 7, 71.
Keep, John, 31.
Keith, Jonathan, 93.
Kilborn, Elijah, 9, 71.
Lathrop, Ichabod, 4, 70.
Lenester, Abigail, 31.
Mansfield, Betsey, 9, 71.
    Fanny, 3.
    Martha, 3.
    Polly, 3.
Markham, Stephen, 93.
Marsh, Reuben, 93.
Merrill, Capt. Abijah, 93.
    Lucy, 93.
Mosier, Freeman, 93.
Mott, Abia, 8, 71.
Munson, Phebe, 16.
Newel, Mary, 9.
    Ruth, 6, 70.
Niblow, Elizabeth, 3.
Northrop, Electa, 70.
    Job, 8, 71.

Atkins, Henry, 78.
Austin, Joseph Freeman, 76.
   Margaret, 76.
   Zafna, 12, 72, 76.
   Zafna, 76.
   Child of James, 72, 76.
   "   "   74, 76.
Backus, Benjamin, 73, 85.
   Deliverance, 12, 72.
   Nathaniel, 87.
   Walley, s. of Walley,
             13.
   Son of Walley, 13.
Baker, Avis, 13.
   Ebenezer, 13.
   Child of David, 13.
Ball, Nathan, 74. 91.
   Sarah, 13. 76.
Barden, see Burden.
Barlow, Cornelius, 72.
   Lydia, 73.
   Child of Reuben, 14,
             72.
   "   " 14. 74.
Bassett, Anner, 73. †
   Annah, 74, 77.
   Harriet, 15, 74, 77.
   John Smith, 15.
   Joseph, 15, 75, 77.
   Mary, 83, 91.
   Nancy, 15, 77.
   Child of Ansel, 14.
   Child of Cornelius, 14.
Beecher, Parmelia, 72, 77.
   Phebe, 77.
   Thomas, 77.
Benedict, Esther, 15.
   Eunice, 15.
   Mary, 15, 87.
   Nathan, 15.
Bennett, Betsey, 15, 77.
   Child of George, 72.
Blackman, Orra, 73.
Bradley, Charity, 16, 87.
   Esther, 83, 87.
   Lydia, 83, 87.
   Child of Jesse Jr., 16.
   Child of Joseph, 16.
Burden, Betsey, 17, 74.
   Meribah, 48, 75.
Casey, Dennis, 47, 74.
   Molly, 46, 73.
   Peggy, 47, 74.
Chadwick, Cynthia, 47, 74.
   Desire, 17, 78.
   Ebenezer, 47, 74.

Chadwick, John, 17.
   Samuel, 17.
   Samuel, 85.   ·
   Child of Caleb, 72.
Chase, Mercy, 18.
   Seth, 18.
   Silence, 47, 74.
   Tabitha, 18.
Church, Daniel, 18.
   Daniel, 18.
   Daniel, 48, 75, 89.
   Daniel, 75, 89.
   Hannah, 18, 89.
Clark, son of Jabez, 72.
   Son of Silas, 73.
Couch, Samuel, 48, 75.
   Sarah, 48, 75.
   Child of John, 48, 75.
Crocker, Abigail, 46, 73, 89.
   Betsey Crosby, 20, 74.
   Content, 72, 78.
   Dorcas, 74.
   Hannah, 45, 72.
   Joseph, son of Joseph
     Jr., 19, 73, 78.
   Joseph Jr., 19, 73, 89.
   Mercy Hamblin, 19,
     73. 78.
   Thomas, 20, 74.
   Capt. Thomas, 46, 73,
     89.
   Zeruiah, 47, 74, 78.
   Child of Josiah, 20.
Crosby, child of John, 20, 72.
   Child of John, 20, 73.
Davis, Hannah, 72, 78.
   Isaac, 91.
   Jedediah, 20.
   Sarah, 20.
Easton, Polly, 22, 72, 78.
Ewer, Lydia, 74.
   Mercy, 22, 72, 79.
   Child of Paul, 72.
Farrar, child, 72.
Finney, Barnabas, 23.
   Benjamin Franklin,
     22.
   Polly, 23.
   Child of Abraham, 22.
Foot, David, 23, 79.
   Jerusha, 24, 87.
   John, 24, 87.
   Sarah, 85.
   William, 24, 72, 87.
   Child of Alvan, 23,
     75, 79.

† Anner in Dr. Hyde's record, but Mary on gravestone

Wilcox, Electa, 48, 75, 83, 87.
     Hudson, 40.
     Jerusha, 41.
     Oziel, 41.
     Peter, Jr., 46.
Williams, Lucy, 82.

Winegar, Caty, 47, 74, 89.
     John, 47, 74, 89.
     Zach, 42, 89.
     Child of Jacob,74,83,89
     Child of Jacob, 83, 89.
Wormer, Mary Ann, 75.
Wyllys, Elizabeth. 42.
     Rhoda, 42.
Youngs, son of James, 72.

ERRATA AND OMISSIONS.

Page 1.   In second publishment, for "Ichabod," read "Ichobud."

Page 10.   In second intention from bottom, for "Polly Ball," read "Patty Ball."

Page 27.   Record regarding Rebecca Hatch doubtless incorrect:—"Rebecca, wife of Mr Oliver Hatch died May 1st 1788". See p. 87. Dates after Polly and Ira Hill, printed as recorded.

In a copy of the 1st vol. of town records, made by Franklin G. Taylor in 1858, is the birth record of Benjamin Hinckley's children with the three dates ~~wanting~~ which are in the original 1st vol. These dates are not in the writing of the copyist, but in that of a town clerk later than 1858.

The record of the copy is:—

Children of Benjamin Hinckley & Puella Goodspeed his wife

Electa Hinkley Born Jan 10. 1787 ["Hinkley," in record.]

Thomas Goodspeed Born Feb 5, 1789.

Warren Hinckley Born April 24. 1795.

Charles Hinckley   Oct. 22, 1800.

Luther Thatcher Hinckley May 2d, 1809.

Page 30.   "Lem¹ ", son of Calvin Ingersoll, indistinct,—may be Lemi. See p. 94 for births of three last of David Ingersoll's children.

Page 50.   Mrs. Jesse Bradley's name incorrectly recorded,—should be Mamry or Mamre (see p. 87).
For "Ruhannah Ball", read "Ruhamah Ball".

Page 51.   For "choose" in second line, read "chose."

Page 59.   In fourth line,—"letters missive from the Church in that place", etc., should be,—"letters missive from the church of Christ in that place", etc.

Page 63.   In baptisms, July 8, for "Elisha son of Lydia Ingersol,"etc., read "Elihu, son of Lydia Ingersol," etc.
In baptisms, Sep. 23, Mrs. Jonathan Foot's name is incorrect in record:—see pp. 24, 87.

N. B. An error was made in ascribing the first part of the first book of church records to Wm. Ingersoll (see pp. 53, 55). A more careful scrutiny of the manuscript shows that it is not in his writing, though closely resembling it. The writer is unknown. The writing stated in the second note p. 55, as supposed to be Deacon Oliver West's has been positively identified as his.

www.ingramcontent.com/pod-product-compliance
Lightning Source LLC
Chambersburg PA
CBHW032102010726
47493CB00008B/2502